KEY WEST, 2720 A.D.

WILLIAM K. EAKINS

Stamford, Connecticut

Copyright © 1989 by William K. Eakins

All rights reserved. No part of this book may be reproduced in any form, without the written permission of the author, except for short quotations for review purposes.

Cover design by Christopher Karukas. ©

Published by Knights Press, P.O. Box 454, Pound Ridge, NY 10576

Distributed by Lyle Stuart, Inc.

Library of Congress cataloging-in-publication Data

Eakins, William.
   Key West 2720 A.D. / by William K. Eakins.
      p.   cm.
   ISBN 0-915175-33-9 : $9.00
   I. Title.
PS3555.A425K4   1989
813'.54—dc19   88-29260
                                                              CIP

Printed in the United States of America

For the late Edward Wallowitch

Who first told me that writers write.

KEY WEST, 2720 A.D.

1

Sam Phoe bolted upright. His entire body shook, and a sticky wetness covered his bare skin. In the cabin's dim, grayish illumination he could see the damage he had done to the light cotton sheet that had covered him; it lay to the side, well twisted, and torn in one corner.

"Whale piss!"

He breathed deeply, forcing unwilling lungs to expand wide and accept cool air. Pulse rate slowing, Sam swung both feet out of bed onto a slightly vibrating floor. His feet sank into a thick pile when he stood. Maybe, if he was lucky, a splash of cold water in the face would help him return to sleep—without the damned dream!

It was always the same: He found himself on a tightrope stretched between two towering granite cliffs with a limitless precipice below him. Wind would swirl and tug the rope as, arms outstretched, he struggled to keep his balance. His body bobbed violently, but he made progress. Safety came nearer. Just as he would approach the far cliff top, a hawk would circle above, at first a shadow and then a screaming in his ears—and there would be a bleeding gash down the side of his face. Balance lost, he would fall. He always awoke before hitting bottom; whether this was a mercy or not lay open to debate.

He stood, swaying slightly: from his own lack of balance

and not the ship's roll and pitch, for her rapid movement atop the sea was nearly undetectable. The head door was two lurches away. By an inch Sam missed stepping on a bright orange, crablike maintenance robot, let out a curse, and plunged into the head.

"Dreams," he mumbled as he pushed cupped hands under a faucet. "How I wish they were merely my mind's demented rumblings."

Water flowed, and he filled his hands, then gave his face a cold, splashing shock. The head's lighting brightened slightly. Its holographic "mirror" altered from a picture of Key West viewed from the sea at night to an image of a tall and worn, white-haired man blinking reddened eyes in the brighter lighting.

The problem, Sam realized, was that he knew exactly what this recurring dream meant. He had struggled for more years than most men lived to keep Key West alive and independent and flourishing in all its bizarre glory. He had done so much ass-licking with the elite of the various city-states and Corporates that his lips had a permanent brown tinge. He flattered these people—most of whom he despised—played one faction against another, bribed . . . well, he did whatever it took to keep Glades off his city's back. This trip had been to Albany City-State for a meeting of the Washington DC Restoration Committee.

"Enlarge. Face left." The holo obliged and gave Sam a close-up of a wrinkle under his left eye. "You're new."

This was the second blemish on an otherwise smooth face in the past year. It worried Sam right now when he didn't need fresh worries. Except for white hair, he looked thirty-five. He had looked thirty-five for a hundred and eighty-two years, since he really had been thirty-five.

"Something new in your life, babe," he whispered to himself. "You're dying. At long last."

When *Bitch in Heat* delivered him to his home island in a few more days, Doc Pulski would get his long-awaited inspection of him. Sam had been dodging Doc for several years, ever since the fellow got it into his head that the world's oldest living human should have a medical record. No way! But now?

The ship swayed slightly, first forward, then backward. She was slowing and coming down off her hydrofoils.

"Time?"

Beside the image of his tan face just to the right of his nose the holo read "05:48 16 FEBRUARY 2720." Without being asked, the system displayed a green locater map in the air below his request. They were a mile off a marshy coast that had once been Georgia, near where ancient Savannah had stood before th oceans rose—an area of disputed ownership between Atlanta and Charlotte, a dangerous place.

"What's the trouble, *Bitch*?"

"GOOD MORNING, SAM," said a sultry female voice. "*I HAVE DETECTED WEAPONS FIRE ALONG THE BEACH. HEAT PATTERNING SUGGESTS A SMALL GROUP PURSUED BY A LARGER ONE. THE LATTER WELL ARMED, THE FORMER UNARMED.*"

"An Excludeds hunt?"

"*IF NOT A HUNT, THEN AN EXTERMINATION PARTY. DO YOU WISH TO SEE?*"

Sam grunted, leaned against the low sink counter, and watched the holo area turn blood red, adjust to a fuzzy gray, then to a clean and crisp 3-D picture of a grass-covered dune. A nearly naked boy, perhaps fourteen, sprinted along the edge between scruffy pines. He halted, looked back. Sam could see the terror in his eyes; it made difficult watching. The boy spotted something and darted out of cover, but tripped and tumbled down into the sand. A grinning man with a face flushed red charged to the berm, raised a handgun, and fired. The boy yelled and writhed under a stream of deadly pellets. Foamy surf, slowly turned red, washed about the youth as the man continued to fire until his weapon emptied, long after the boy had died.

Sam jerked his gaze from the holo; his heart was pounding, and a slow fury burned the tips of his ears. "How many are still alive?"

"ONLY TWO, SAM. I'M SORRY."

All Sam Phoe needed right now was to get Atlanta or Charlotte pissed at him. They would complain to Glades, and Glades would lean on Key West. And besides, what if one of the claimants of this real estate had aircraft in the vicinity?

To hell with it!

"*Bitch*, distract the pursuers. Then lay down laser fire to cut them off from their prey. And get Brio the hell out of bed!"

"YES, SAM."

He could detect a light hum as his ship diverted power to her laser cannon. Those bastard hunters were about to get one hell of a surprise.

As he left the head, Sam grabbed a pair of pants from where he had tossed them, over a wall-hung brass lamp, flopped on the bed, and pulled both legs up at once. Black knee boots followed. His shirt he had thrown in the recycle, so he yelled at the paneled wall, "A shirt and cape for off ship. Something rugged."

Seconds later the insets on the far bulkhead hummed aside as a selection of clothing on wire racks was pushed out at him. Sam stood and wiggled his feet into the boots to get a better fit, then walked to the closet rack. The mechanism offered him four shirts and two capes, one long, one short. He chose a loose raven pull-over, whose shiny black winked at him, and a full white cape. The device beeped and shoved a second undershirt of a thin silvery material at him and refused to stop beeping until he took the armor cloth.

"Nag!"

He snatched the thing, pulling it over his head, feeling a shiver from its cold touch. As he put on and tucked in the black shirt, Sam moved about his cabin collecting things he might need: a pouch of small gold coins that tinkled as he handled it, for despite a desire to fry the boarder guards who so mercilessly killed, he would have to bribe them instead; and a horse-head walking cane that concealed an arsenal.

Dressed, he stood dead still for a moment and rubbed at a small scar on his chin, reviewing what tactic he might use with these men—greed, of course, for one thing or another. Gold was not always enough. He moved to a bronze end table that adjoined a long couch and placed his thumb atop a white tile set into its surface. A drawer slid open. Rummaging in it, he at last located a tiny ear plug, tiny but valuable; it was a data link capable of direct contact with the Corporate's main computer centers. No one who was a border guard would ever hope to own such a device; its possession could well lead to better things than chasing Excludeds through coastal marshlands. He shoved it in a shirt pocket.

The cabin door slid aside as he approached. He entered a wide hall of shiny oak paneling. The passageway smelled of wood polish and new carpeting. Brio Dirrenni, his aide aboard *Bitch*, was nowhere in sight though Sam heard some muffled scrapping coming from aft, the direction he strode. Aft lay the sealed launching bay for the ship's omnicraft.

At his approach, the door into Brio's small cabin slid open. There stood the dark-haired young man fighting with the zipper on his jump suit. Sam's gaze snapped to a view of white undershorts barely restraining a massive hard-on, the rosy head of which was displayed against tawny skin as it stuck out above the waist band.

Oh! *Not now*, he thought.

Brio looked up and grinned. The large nose from his Italian ancestry gave his face a look more playful and boyish than handsome. But his physique lacked nothing and could have decorated any forum or temple.

"Having trouble with high-tech devices?" Sam gibed.

Brio snorted. The zipper unstuck and traveled to his navel, where it was abandoned, leaving midriff and chest to entice Sam. He felt like a diabetic in a candy store. Sam wanted

Brio, but Sam also knew what Brio wanted: an escalator ride to Whitehead Palace and not a pleasant tryst in bed. No, no! Sam's household was too big already, and sleeping with fellow islanders had become too problem-filled.

They left the cabin, moved the last twenty feet between them and the hall's aft bulkhead, and passed through into the brightly lighted launch bay, a place of curving white walls with but one egg-shaped piece of equipment centered in it. This was *Whelp II*, an omnicraft. Sam could smell the sharp scent of ozone as *Bitch* charged the craft's weapons.

There was no sensation of movement now, for the ship had stopped and lay submerged just below the surface with only her cannon and conning tower above water. Sam could almost taste the silence. Seconds became minutes, but at last *Whelp II*'s smooth white surface formed a seam. A section moved inward and aside to reveal a blue-glowing interior.

They scurried inside, Brio entering first and taking one of the rear seats with its own control panel. All Sam noticed, as he came through the hatch and took the forward pilot's chair, was Brio's pointed brown nipples visible as he bent slightly to affix a seat harness. This close, the young man's body odor wafted to him: a fresh herbal scent as though he had just stepped out of the shower. Sam, on the other hand, always smelled like a musk ox in August with the least exertion. He sniffed at himself; not too bad now.

"Shame you don't have a few of the Fundy Guard along," Brio said, against a loud background whine.

"Then even those idiots would know who we are!"

Sam felt a series of vibrations as the omnicraft altered its shape around them, as it became a boat rather than a land vehicle or an aircraft. He concentrated for a second so that his mind could locate its control link with *Bitch*. It opened with the familiar, and unpleasantly acrid, taste of copper on the back of his tongue.

You there, Bitch?

YES, SAM.
Take us ashore, with as few bumps as possible!
I HAVE OPENED FIRE. THE BORDER GUARDS ARE TAKING COVER, SAM.

He hated communicating using a brainlink. Each contact left him with a headache the size of Atlanta and no palate for food for days. Given this, the idea of a full link, where he and his computers functioned as one, had appealed to him about as much as death.

They were jarred about slightly as *Whelp II* launched.

"Say, Sam, is this butchering of Excludeds something new?"

He sighed. "Revived. And I'm not sure why. Hacker tells me the Excluded tribes have pulled way back from most of the city-states. Look how far this hunt is from either Atlanta or Charlotte! Glades is behind it!"

Reaching a finger down to the illuminated array of symbols on the control panel, Sam poked for a view outside. The curving wall before him dissolved into iron-colored water and violent wave as *Whelp II* cleared to the surface. The coast formed a thin grayish band at midscreen; it was still half a mile in. Sunrise was more imagined than real, for the craft's computer adjusted the lighting to his visual limits. Reality was still dark.

Sam continued, "The cities used to kill traitors rather than exclude them . . . but gays—well, if a boy failed the hormone test they'd hand him a bag of clothing and a week's food. Goodbye, queer! He either makes it among the wandering tribes, or he dies.

"Glades is pushing extermination, Brio, and I have nightmares from not knowing why!"

Sam thought about Brio's history. He had been dumped at Key West as a boy of thirteen by a father broken-hearted at producing a son *Il Duce* would not allow to remain inside the walls of Rome. The man had thought enough of the boy not to want him sent to the pleasure houses at Tivoli—or perhaps he couldn't stomach the idea of compliments from his colleagues on how good a blow job his son gave. At least Rome City-State had a use for gays, though political opponents weren't so "lucky." But Brio had been bright and affable, had pledged to Walt's Fraternity and was accepted. He had blossomed. But gays they had rescued from Excluded status often lived out shortened lives hiding from human contact.

Bitch, *they still keeping their heads low?* Sam opened the link to clear thoughts of a subject that raised his blood pressure. Some part of him might order those border agents vaporized—unwise.

I HAVE BLOCKED THEIR RADIO CHANNELS, BUT I AM TRANSMITTING YOUR DESIRE TO DO BUSINESS. DO YOU WISH TO HEAR THEIR REPLY LIVE?

Sam sent a mental image of puke in answer to *Bitch*'s question. Sometimes words weren't adequate.

Gibb could not run much farther; his muscles screamed at him, and his lungs took in fire. Dry beach sand made each sinking step drain his will to survive. Kao was behind him somewhere. And so were the hunters. He heard shots and cringed, awaiting the pain in his back. None came. He plunged on, dodging into a stand of pine just off the dune top. Small cones crunched under foot. He turned his head back and looked into the steel gray of early morning. Where was his friend?

"Run, Kao, run," Gibb whispered.

Then there was no ground under him.

Gibb's stomach fell away. A second later he splashed into frozen water. Salt lined his mouth, and he had trouble breathing around the pain in his chest and liquid in his nose. A fit of coughing drained what energy remained in his body.

He sat waist deep in a mixture of salt water, dead grass, leaves, and slime. Thin shoots of some plant stuck straight up, jabbing into his bare legs. Standing to either side of him, tall and well-rooted sand banks defined the marshy creek he had fallen into, a reward for not watching where his feet went. However, he spotted hope near the top of the cliff he had tumbled over.

Fast summer rain flows had deeply undercut the bank about two-thirds of the way up, forming a dark opening bearded by coarse grass roots, invisible from above on the dune top. It looked like a great dark eye, with eyebrow, staring down at him.

Gibb found enough energy to crawl from the cold water; he scrabbled at the sandy bank, winning a way upward by digging his hands and arms in nearly to the elbows. Every three feet up he lost two, but at last tumbled under the hanging roots and into the opening, hoping as he did so that it wasn't a den for some badger—or cottonmouth!

The hole swallowed him. Grains of sand sprinkled down into his curly hair. A pungent odor of damp vegetation overpowered him, pushing away the sea smells. His skin burned from various abrasions and cuts, now irritated by salt. Once still again, his body began to shake and tremble from the strain of two days' continuous running, from months of fear, and from a chilling cold that seemed lifelong.

A thumping from running feet vibrated down to him. They were close!

"I'm worm food," he whispered.

A scream of pain and agony tore into Gibb's dark hole. Pealing laughter and loud whoops followed.

"Oh, Kao. I'm sorry." Gibb remembered the yellow-haired younger boy with his wide grin, his warmth beside him on cold nights in the mountains. He and Kao had been together since his tribe, the Peakers, had been ambushed in the Alleghenys last summer. A memory of steel death machines shooting fire sent another chill down his spine, one unrelated to the cold dampness about him. Never had any tribe been attacked like that, or so old Strongfoot had related before he died of winter fever. Of the hundred men, women, and children who had formed his new family, who had taken him in after Charlotte . . . after the city had tossed him out, only twelve escaped those robot tanks. They had been chased ever since. Now, likely, he was alone again.

A sob shook him.

By reflex now, whenever fear overcame him, Gibb reached into his pocket, past the sand, and brought out a thin disc of metal. It was pure silver, about the size of a large acorn. He could not see its shiny surface, for the inside of his hiding place was nearly black. The coin lacked the symbols or pictures, being smooth on both sides, that most city coins had, but he remembered the man who had given it to him. That man had brought food—and lots of it!—two winters back. The Peakers would have eaten some of their own and still likely have died without the man's help.

Gibb rubbed the metal between thumb and forefinger, feeling its soothing smoothness and remembering the tall, powerfully built man who had given it. He had worn a short beard the color of autumn maple leaves and a smile that gave meaning to the world. Gibb remembered his soft words spoken late one night:

"Take this, son, in case you need extra supplies from the traders before we can return to your tribe. And remember, you do have friends."

Gibb had asked, "Which city do you come from?" for the man was clearly a city-lord.

The man shook his head, but placed an arm about him—Gibb remembered a wave of desire that was never fulfilled. The city-lord seemed to reflect a moment about answering him, then turned a smile toward Gibb and slowly pointed at the star-filled sky.

Gibb's whimpering stomach brought him back to the certain death he faced. A cold wind, forcing its way in to him and laced with the scent of salt and seaweed, moaned just outside.

He returned the coin to his pocket and began digging furiously about in the sand wall of his hiding place, tearing first at one wall, then another. At last he found a pointed scrap of driftwood the length of his forearm. It would have to do.

"God, I'm tired of running from death. I ask only one small favor. Let me kill one of them first—just one!" *One for Kao, Lord*, he prayed.

Gibb stuck his head out from the hole; its draping roots tickled his face. Clutching the stake in one hand, using it to aid his climb up the sand cliff, he worked to within a yard of the top. Footsteps he heard, and they were close.

Bright red light suddenly illuminated the entire beach and gully like midday in July.

He thought that his pursuers used flares to locate him, then a crack deafened him, pushing out the roar of surf and leaving a ringing in his ears. Slowly, his eyes again formed pictures without bloody patches, and his ears stopped pulsing. A dancing yellow light flooded over the cliff; pops and hissing filled the air along with yelling and curses, coming from atop the dune. He edged up. The sand gave way; he slid down six feet before catching a root end. Feeling and stabbing his way up more carefully this time, Gibb at last gazed over the edge. White, resinous smoke blew in his face and choked him. The trees blazed.

He coughed, hoped no one heard him. Beyond the drifting clouds of smoke and soot, he could see the hunters, hunched down on the beach, pointing out to sea, well lighted by the burning stand of pines. They were afraid. That warmed Gibb's heart. He might have a chance at one of them while they were distracted.

Grayness had become a wan half-light. Out to sea, beyond the breakers, something moving caught Gibb's eye. At first he thought hunger was making him see things that weren't there. Then terror twisted his heart. A robot machine!

The thing was bigger than three wagons and walked on six multijointed legs, three to each side. Its silvery body reminded

Gibb of a chicken egg except that part of its upper surface formed a bulge to the front, out from which stuck several short tubes. The hunters' reaction to the machine was clearly fear: they kept fidgeting and ducking down and muttering curses. Their attentions were fixed.

Gibb crawled up onto the dune top and bellied his way into the cordgrass. It cut his chest and made the rest of his skin itch. His fingers ached from the grip he kept on the makeshift dagger.

When he came to an opening in the stands of grass, Gibb could again see the machine, now resting flat on the upper dune, legs hunched up to its sides. It shone reddish pink as dawn lit its reflective surface. Gibb wiggled closer, stopping when he came to within thirty feet of one hunter, a squat man dressed in a ragged tan uniform. A hum from the machine forced Gibb's attention back to it.

One side of the thing had opened and a man climbed out. He was tall, thin, and his hair was the color of new snow, slightly reddened by the beginning of dawn. Dressed in black and white, the fellow strode toward the hunters, halting a few paces from them. There existed no doubt in Gibb's mind: the man was a high city-lord, his every movement and commanding gesture proved it; perhaps he came from Gibb's birthplace of Charlotte. His conversation with the hunters was fiery. Gibb could hear only every third word or so for the wind blew from the north and pushed the sound away from him.

"You have . . . no . . . to interfere . . . ," one of the forwardmost hunters said, gesticulating wildly. The city-lord stood like a statue, leaning on a stick he carried. The man's white cape tossed lightly in the wind. After the hunter ran down, the lord pulled a pouch from his pocket and tossed it to the lead hunter. Their words came to Gibb as mutters, but pleased mutters.

What's going on, he wondered?

However, once again the lead hunter grunted, waved his

hands, and pointed back over his shoulder. The city-lord took something else from a pocket and held it up between thumb and forefinger. Whatever this was exicted the men more than the first gift had. They laughed. A gusting southeaster brought Gibb a few words:

". . . I know," said the lead hunter, chuckling, "you got access to the organ buyers. We hearda them. Just we never could get none of these animals to 'em! Cut 'em up for parts—get some use out o' 'em, hey!"

The city-lord remained stone-faced, but a new flavor of fear began to fill Gibb. *They're bargaining for me*! he thought, and began to inch away from the scene, back toward a dirt hole they might not find.

He had crawled twenty feet when something moved near the path he took. Gibb looked at a pair of black boots, then up into the intense face of the city-lord staring down at him. The man offered a hand up. He took it without ever allowing his gaze to leave the lord's thin face with its bushy white eyebrows. The man was a foot taller than he.

"Come along, boy. My ship's waiting, and these vermin give me the heaves."

Gibb followed the man, perhaps to death. But he couldn't force one thought from his mind: if God had a face, it would look exactly like this city-lord's.

Sam Phoe took a sip of his afternoon tea and drew his face into a pucker; *Bitch* had made it too strong again. Giving a mental shrug, he moved through his cabin's head, and out into the den located on its far side, taking the porcelain cup with him. A retractable bed jutted from the far wall. The Excluded boy lay there attended by Brio, who applied a drug patch to one arm. The boy was asleep.

It had been weeks since Sam had used this cabin, a place he liked to hide from the current world and read ancient bound books, which lined one wall. A small robot device crawled along the shelves, silently removing dust and polishing the shelf edges. An encased collection of antique swords and daggers hung on the wall over the bunk.

"How is our newest citizen?" Sam asked Brio.

The youth looked up with a wide grin on his face, wiped a strand of black hair from in front of his eyes. "How can ya be so sure he qualifies? I mean he could be a tribal native, a political reject—or whatever, and straight as an arrow."

Sam looked down at the boy. He was eighteen, give or take, but he was small and looked much younger, a side effect of malnutrition. His ribs stuck out too prominently, and most of his bare body looked emaciated; yet he was well-muscled and his skin glowed with an even tan. Beneath a tangle of curly black hair lay a narrow face with a squarish jaw and lips so thick as to demand a kiss.

"Whale piss!"

Brio chuckled. "You're right. Blood work puts him well into the gay range. Patch," he pointed at the tiny orange circle he had pasted on the boy's arm, "is for worms. Had quite a collection."

Sam shuddered. Snakes and even microscopic worms he liked to keep well away from. Once in his life he had lived with too many of them. "Drug sleep?"

"Naw. Got him showered. Then gave him a bottle of liquid nutrient. Minute he finished that—out!" Brio stood and walked to a nearby tub chair and flopped down. "His name's Gibb."

Gibb, Sam thought as he seated himself on the edge of the bed. One hand he put on the boy's chest, with a finger of the other hand he traced Gibb's jaw. His skin was cool, and surprisingly, soft and smooth like the finest glove leather. But from earlier, on the beach, Sam remembered the dark eyes, eyes far too big for his face.

I would have looked like that, taller, but I would have looked just like that when the Colonel found me, Sam thought. It had been the winter of 2520—two hundred years ago this year! he suddenly realized—the fifth year of his exclusion, and the worst winter he'd ever experienced.

He remembered crawling up a long incline, reaching a steep-sided col atop a ridge to gain a look down into the white-blanketed Ohio River Valley, just to see the home he had lost at age twelve: Cincinnati City-State. He remembered a two minute glimpse at its blue-tinted dome, interior towers and green parks before a clicking had startled him, too late.

The machine was a multiclawed personal transporter and it had netted him, had him well trussed up ready for roasting. That city-staters ate tribal people was a myth of the mountain peoples. They didn't, of course. The tribes were excluded and left to the eating of worms, when they could find such good fare, which wasn't in winter.

A man with rosy cheeks and a one-side grin, dressed in a thick, bright red jump suit had climbed out of that machine. Sam had kicked and torn at the immovable netting, had spit at his captor. The fellow stood and watched until Sam had run down, had resigned himself to being eaten.

Then the man popped the netting loose. "Come along, boy," he had said. It may have been the man's tone, but Sam had followed him up into the transporter. Rather ingloriously, but that was how Sam's twelve-year association with the Colonel and his infamous band of mercenaries began. The unit was named the Queen's Brigade. It was composed of youths and young men, every one gay, that the Colonel had collected from all over the northeast. Some outsiders thought that the Colonel had a taste for young men and wanted a harem along with his business. No. The Colonel was straight, much to Sam's chagrin.

The summer after he began training with the Colonel's men, the Third City-States War had erupted. Business thrived during that decade as great city after great city went up in radioactive smoke until only thirteen remained within the old

USA's territory. Sam had no sympathy whatsoever. When it had ended, Sam was twenty-seven, a major, and second in command of the Queens' Brigade. Then Glades decided to hire extra soldiers to finish off its archrival, the fanatically religious World City-state, in central Florida . . . .

"Sam. Sam, did you hear a word I said?" Brio stood beside him proffering a small disc of metal.

"Of course I did. What's this?" He set his teacup on a nightstand nearby and took it. The coin was cold to the touch.

Brio looked at the ceiling and sighed. "Gibb there gave it to me—to quote: for his safe passage."

Sam turned it over in the palm of his hand. "Does he think this is a ferry?"

Brio chuckled, Sam snorted.

"Put some clothes on him," Sam ordered.

But Brio grinned all the wider. "I thought you'd want him that way for a private inspection."

Glaring up at the youth, Sam Phoe rose from the bed. Brio's grin faded as Sam backed him into a corner. He placed a large hand on each of the young man's wide shoulders. "Are you implying that I take my pleasure with half-dead, unconscious boys?"

"No! No . . . Mayor Phoe, sir!" Brio stuttered.

Sam could feel the young man shiver as he narrowed his eyes and stuck his face so close to Brio's that their noses nearly touched. "Do you know what I do to twenty-year-old, impudent kids?"

Beads of sweat were forming on Brio's tawny neck as he shook his head.

Backing off the youth, Sam spun about, and returned to stand by the bed. "I ignore them."

He heard Brio expel a long-held breath, then quietly slink from the cabin. Sam bent over and opened a drawer under the bed and pulled out a light, open-weave blanket. He tossed it over the sleeping boy.

The silver piece still lay on the side of the bed where he had tossed it. Retrieving it, he again looked at both blank sides, but with a milled edge—it was a unit of money. He stepped over to the table centered in the den and set the coin down. "Well?"

The table's surface glowed for a second.

"ONE QUARTER OUNCE SILVER, PURE TO TWELVE DECIMAL PLACES: EQUAL TO FIVE DOLLARS," replied *Bitch*.

"Who would refine coin silver that pure?"

"*I AM NOT HACKER, SAM.*" *Bitch* sounded testy.

No, Sam thought, and—damn it!—Hacker is still off-line for some reason. And *Bitch* was angry with him. Discontented cyberbrains were a real hazard.

"What's wrong?"

"*BRIO IS SITTING IN HIS CABIN WITH THE LIGHTS OUT.*"

To order *Bitch* to mind her own business was a faulty argument bordering the stupid. Every aspect of their lives while aboard the ship was her business—even pouting aides!

"I'll kiss him and make up. Okay?"

"SOMETIMES, SAM, YOU FORGET THAT IN THE MINDS OF KEY WESTERS YOU APPROACH SAINTHOOD. YOUR WORDS CAN BE DEVASTATING, EVEN IF THEY ARE SPOKEN IN JEST."

"Whale piss!" Saints always got unwanted objects stabbed into their bodies. Sam eschewed sainthood.

He retrieved the coin, pocketed it, but stared at the analysis on the tabletop screen. It listed two pollutants at that thirteenth decimal place: carbon and iridium. The silver had been mined in deep space.

2

"Damn!" A dribble of yoke from his poached egg dropped onto the table screen Sam had been reading—a fitting comment on what he saw there. He used his napkin to wipe up the yellow goo and glanced up at his companions. Gibb picked at his breakfast, inspecting each item with his fork, then taking a small bite with his egg-yoke-covered fingers as if he thought they were going to poison him. The boy looked up from time to time with eyes that could melt the soul of Attilla the Hun. Still, they were eyes awash with fear. Cleaned up, his appearance was so androgynous that Sam's mind could even picture him pregnant. He credited that odd image to another restless night of dreamed tightrope walking.

"How's the grub?" he asked the boy, giving his biggest smile.

"Strange—but good, lord."

"Lord" as a title wouldn't go over too well on the island; he would have to break the boy of that habit. "Gibb, please call me 'Sam.'"

Gibb blinked, nodded, and gazed back at the plate of poached eggs on eggplant.

Brio stared into his coffee, still pouting.

Sam returned his attention to less than propitious news: Kenton White had been elected Speaker of the Assembly.

Key West, 2720 A.D.

Once every generation for the past four generations Sam had been forced to defend his position as Mayor of Key West, an office held at the pleasure of the Assembly. What made this battle especially irksome was his relationship with White: They were ex-lovers and, technically, still married. And Kenton had a new tactic. He missed no opportunity to call Sam Phoe a dictator, the conqueror of Key West! White had the nerve to say that the Fundy Guard cast fifty-one per cent of any vote!

His ears were beginning to burn from these thoughts, so he touched the screen for a new subject. In Uriel Fordac's usual brevity, a note stated that four secret police agents from Glades had arrived on the island the evening before. Nothing unusual in that, but they put a pall on any place they went. Key West had its own way of dealing with such unwelcome visitors: a Fundy accompanied each agent wherever he went, whether he liked it or not. Like painting a chameleon's tail bright orange.

Welcome news! His hotel, the Da Vinci, was full. Even dictatorial mayors had to pay their bills—or Narlo Adamms's bills!

He took a bit of his brioche, washing it down with a sip of tea—too weak this time, one of *Bitch*'s few failings. A flashing square of red appeared on the screen. He thumbed for the message:

> I WANT TO SEE YOU AT ONCE. ON YOUR WAY SOUTH, FLY INTO MY OFFICE AT TWENTY-MILE.
>
> **SUDGER.**

Sam felt the brioche try to crawl back up his throat. He let out a belch. Jacksen Lear Sudger III always made him wish he had developed suicidal tendencies, for then he could have simply murdered the man. He would instruct *Bitch* to notify New Havana, Albany, and a few other cities that he was going to visit Glades so that Sudger or some of his henchmen wouldn't be tempted to make him vanish. With any luck, he wouldn't have to stay overnight.

Sam looked up to see Brio staring at him; apparently his feelings about a meeting with the President of Glades showed on his face. "Have to visit Glades."

"I'll come with you."

Sam shook his head. He glanced halfway down the long table to where Gibb sat, sipping some orange juice from a tumbler that the table had just raised up beside his plate. He still had not questioned the boy about himself or the odd silver coin.

"Gibb, have you ever flown?" Sam asked.

The boy's gaze snapped to him. Terror shone in his eyes as he slowly shook his head. He had turned whiter. Could thoughts of traveling in an aircraft frighten him so much?

Sam glanced up at the crystal chandelier; it swayed slightly as *Bitch* slowed the pace south in preparation for launching *Whelp*. By now they were off the coast of central Florida, and Twenty-Mile, the halfway point along the Oceanway Channel between the sea and Glades, was about thirty minutes away by air.

Rising from his chair, Sam reached down and tapped Gibb's shoulder. The boy jumped. "You'll like flying. Really."

Brio's face, Sam noticed, couldn't decide on an emotional expression: anger, worry, disgust, and disappointment appeared in rapid succession. Sam left the dining room with Gibb in tow; an arm about the boy's shoulders detected mild trembling. Perhaps Sam had forgotten just how terrifying the transition from exclusion back into the civilized world could be. A tiny flame from well-banked sexual coals licked up at him; he removed his arm. The boy followed him down the hallway past a spiral staircase, leading to an upper deck, and through the door into the launching bay.

The omnicraft stood with its hatch open, waiting for them. Sam allowed Gibb to enter first and take the second of two front pilot chairs. When they were seated, protective webbing snaked across them. As the hatch shut, all the console instruments flashed on at once, causing Gibb to jump. Sam touched a square on the console and an area map flashed into view, replacing various multicolored status readouts. He touched Twenty-Mile, while reaching to deactivate *Whelp II*'s defense systems. They were useless against Glades, and that city's military might decide to tease him.

Gibb let out a small yelp when *Bitch* dropped the omnicraft out of her bay.

The front screen provided a lifelike view of bubbles and greenish water. A ray of some kind darted out of their way. In a second they broke surface. Knowing what would happen next, he reached over and gripped one of Gibb's clammy hands. The boy watched on the side screens as the craft formed blunt wings from its rounded hull. A thin whine told Sam that *Whelp II*'s pumps forced air into its fusion-heated jet tubes.

An invisible hand rammed him into the seat; sparkling azure replaced everything else on the screen.

When they reached an altitude of four thousand feet and a speed of six hundred miles per hour, *Whelp II* leveled off. Sam glanced over at Gibb, who had his eyes clamped shut, and tapped the boy's shoulder. He blinked those enormous eyes open, then widened them at what he saw. The forward screen had split its view so that half displayed blue sky with giant cottony clouds and the other half revealed the forest and crop-covered landscape of South Florida below them. *Bitch in Heat* and ocean had been left far behind during their first seconds of flight. They moved southwesterly over the land too fast to observe much detail; in one vast grove of orange trees, however, reflected light from shiny-surfaced picker robots sparkled up at them.

"Relax, Gibb. You look like someone on his way to execution."

The boy's frightened gaze darted to Sam's face, then

jumped back to the view below.

"That silver coin, the one you gave Brio, how did you come by it?"

"Uh . . . I found it, sir."

A dead end, thought Sam.

Sam felt his stomach float up as the craft dropped slightly. In the status panel, a flow of orange letters detailed landing instructions already being sent to *Whelp*, though they were still twenty minutes away. To the right of this display the now toothless defense system provided a proximity diagram of the air space around them. They were being followed.

At ten miles out the screen indicated a fuzzy object that became two fuzzy objects as Sam watched. A radar blip like that meant only one thing: a flight of small cybermissiles. Glades trusted him about as much as he trusted it. He often wondered if it was possible to reason with a cybermissile; in this case they likely had the personality of their owners, so why bother?

Sam was beginning to miss something. The airways this close to Glades should have been thick with an argosy of gas-filled, globular floater craft delivering or picking up goods. There were none.

The Oceanway Channel appeared in the distance, a silver slash in a flat and deep green landscape. He turned to point out this mile-wide waterway to Gibb and felt something prick his neck.

"What the—!"

Gibb spoke with a low but trembling voice. "I don't want to hurt you. But nobody's goin' to cut me up for spare parts, sir."

Sam tried to ask a question, but the knife point discouraged it. Where had the boy gotten an idea like that? Of course! He must have heard what the border guards had said. When Sam had been an Excluded it was the common myth that city folk ate captured Excludeds, now it was that they became unwilling organ donors! Silly, that form of medical treatment had fallen into disuse four hundred years ago. He could feel the start of an ache in his neck from holding one position too long.

The boy went on, "Tell this thing to land. I'll take my chances in the fields. Do it now, sir!"

If Sam overrode the instructions sent by Twenty-Mile's air traffic system, Glades would indulge its paranoia. He might well get the chance to discuss morals with a cybermissile! While touching several areas of the screen in a meaningless sequence to stall for thinking time, Sam at last realized what he must do. Kill the boy.

Sweat creeped down his neck as he opened his brain-link and again experienced the pseudotaste of copper on the back of his tongue. Guilt over this would haunt him a long while; why hadn't he taken the time to sit down with Gibb and talk out the boy's obvious terrors? Those immense eyes would show up in new nightmares.

Cobra, he thought, to activate injection guns located in the seat of each couch. *Two*, he thought, to define which couch.

Dose? Whelp II asked back.

But "dose" had never been an option before! *Bitch* had altered the programming of her offspring. The great Samuel Phoe had just been taught a morals lesson by a machine!

Immobilize! Sam's mind yelled.

The prick of steel at his neck bobbed, cutting him slightly. He reached up and pried the weapon from Gibb's paralyzed hand. Glancing at the knife, he let out a grunt; it was a thin-bladed dagger with lion-head pommel, fifteenth century Venetian, from his collection hanging in the ship's den. He tossed it on the floor.

"Sam, how have you stayed alive this long?" he asked himself.

Looking up, Sam stared into a frozen face. Muscles in the boy's jaw twitched, and his eyes stared wide open, seeing the world and the terror it held for him, simply unable to move.

Shortly he would be unconscious. What could Sam do this time so that fear didn't again bring tragedy so close?

He reached a hand behind Gibb's neck, pulled him closer, and kissed the youth on his pouty lips. Backing away, Sam smiled and saw the boy's still face relax. A second later he closed his eyes and slumped to one side.

The way my luck runs, Sam thought, you're going to be my next lover: I've got one who's trying to spend me into the ground, one who's trying to kick me off the island—now all I'm missing is one who tries to knife me every other day!

"Well, Gibb," he said aloud, "you've lost your one and only chance to spit in the eye of Jacksen Lear Sudger the Third!"

He reached a hand up to the console on the cabin ceiling, opened a tiny hatch marked by a green cross, and took out a tube of restorative gel. Squeezing a little of the gray goo onto his finger, he rubbed it into his neck wound—its knitting effect tickled his skin—finishing the job by wiping the dried blood away with a handkerchief from his jacket pocket.

"Health status, number two?" he requested of *Whelp*.

A section of screen before him, which had been a blurred view of orange trees, altered to a set of standard graphs for human biofunction. Sam noted those few areas in the red—body weight, blood sugar—as not due to his poisoning the boy. Gibb was merely asleep.

Sam returned a panorama of the outside to the screen when *Whelp II* began to descend. She followed the flickering silver band of the Oceanway Channel, darting over only one giant, wake-tailed freighter. Traffic, even in the canal, was slow indeed. The sun lay directly ahead—not a likely position for morning! He grinned at himself, realizing that Glades had turned on its mirror shield and was throwing the easterly sunlight back at him. As he watched, the optical field dome snapped off and yellow sun was replaced by looming gray spires backdropped by farther distanced jet black thunderheads.

Glades. Still some twenty miles off, westward.

At four hundred and fifty years old, it was the newest city-state on Earth. US AgriCorp began it in AD 2279 to try and reclaim the ocean-flooded agricultural lands of South Florida once the waters had begun their retreat fifty years before. Now, with over two million inhabitants, it was one of the largest and most powerful cities on the planet, reaching its control to ownership of mining colonies on the Moon, Mars, and even the deep space projects such as those on Titan.

The brutalest policies against the Excludeds, gay and otherwise, originated at Glades for reasons he could not fathom. These policies denied logic; Excludeds had ceased to be any threat to the city-states hundreds of years before; where once there had been thirty Excludeds for every city dweller, there were now three city-staters for every Excluded. But he did know the architect of this policy: Jacksen Lear Sudger III.

For Sam Phoe, Glades's policy of cruel extinction against the wandering tribes of rejects had been costly in dignity and gold. Fifteen years of whispering against Glades in Corporate leaders' ears while sucking ass with them had left him feeling depressed and undesirous of human company. When wholesale murder began, he spent several fortunes opening the northerly keys to colonies of transplanted Excludeds—gays went to the main island, as they always had, while straights settled on Sugarloaf and Cudjoe. All this had reduced his personal fortune to the point where he actually needed some of Key West's tax money, leaving him an easy target for Kenton White.

Sam jumped. *Whelp II* had stopped her forward motion and settled hissingly downward amidst twirling dust and grass particles. He closed his eyes and took deep breaths; his neck and shoulder muscles were still tense from his near miss with Gibb.

"Where the hell are we, *Whelp*? This isn't Twenty-Mile!"

The omnicraft overlaid the view of dust swirls with a map.

It had landed a mile south of the Oceanway and Twenty-Mile in an area undefined and marked "restricted."

He tapped a key and the hatch slid back. Real dust floated in, and he coughed. The rich smell of growing vegetation flowing about him gave a nearly overpowering jolt to his senses.

"Whale piss!" he cursed under his breath as he saw a short, pot-bellied figure waiting for him on a slight mound of grassy surface some thirty feet from where *Whelp II* had landed. He stood in front of a massive concrete building with all the architectural character of a beggar's tombstone—a new defense installation of some sort, Sam guessed.

He climbed out of *Whelp* and stretched.

Roscoe Thorsel, Sudger's cousin, strode over to him. A grin tightened his jowls. "Hello, Phoe. How's things in fag city?"

Sam nodded toward the giant building behind the man. "New defense work? You mean to tell me there's somebody who doesn't like Glades?"

The man snorted, began a retort, chewed at his lip a second as a worried look crossed his face. "Mister Sudger's waiting on you."

The spongy grass mound led up to the beginning of a vast plaza before the building, which measured at least a hundred yards to the side and twice that high. A tiny doorway marked the only variation in acres of plain stone surface. A chill easterly wind moaned as it swept around the structure, trying its best to push the building over. Through the door lay a cubic room with walls lined by glowing data screens that displayed continuously changing multicolored diagrams. Sudger sat in the middle of the room, reading from a data plate in his lap while tapping a stylus against his jet black hair. He raised his head as they approached. Sam had always conceded that the man was one of the most handsome he knew, smooth even features, porcelainlike skin, dignified angled cheekbones. The man's iron-gray eyes revealed something else: they were arctic, lacking any human warmth.

"Here's the chief fag—" Thorsel began. Sudger silenced him with a jerk of the hand.

Short and tubby Thorsel, Sam knew, talked a good game; his commitment to fag baiting was one molecule deep and pure ass-lick. Sudger's hatred for gays, on the other hand, was just a little shallower than the Marannas Trench. He wasn't sure why. Perhaps, when the man was younger, his beauty had proven too much of a temptation for someone.

"I have no time for you now, so I'll come right to the point." He aimed the stylus at Sam. "We have information that agents from the Titan miners are in Key West negotiating with our opponents on the Council of Corporates."

This news floored Sam, but he tried not to let it show on his face. He could have named a thousand things he might expect Sudger to dig at him about—this wasn't even on the list!

The President of Glades and Chairman of US AgriCorp continued, "I will assume you know about this—"

Sam raised both hands, palms out. "Honest. It's news to me!"

"—and I'll issue this warning. That distant uprising threatens the ascendancy of all the Corporates—whether the others see it or not! And, if you aid them in any way, all the ass-licking you do in New Havana and Albany won't keep me from leveling your private Sodom! Am I clear?" Sudger folded his arms across his broad chest.

Sam felt a shiver pass up his spine. He had paid almost no attention to the conflict involving Saturn's ninth moon. It had grown out of near-slavery conditions maintained by Solsys Corporation at the colonies there. He knew that Glades owned a quarter of Solsys, which didn't say much for the company's human rights policies. He also knew that the rebellion had spread over the last five years. But Key West involved!

"Most clear, Mister Sudger. May I go now?"

The man's gray eyes surveyed him a moment, then, with a tossing of his wrist, he dismissed Sam and returned to his data plate.

Back outside, Thorsel said, "Oh, Sammy. Don't you all worry about the boss destroying those pretty buildings of yours —especially Whitehead Palace! See, I want Key West for myself somethin' fierce! See, I'll just go in and delete the fags and have a real nice place to run. See?"

The man expected some retort from Sam, but Sam's mind remained with a reshuffling of his worldview; a joker had been played, and he had no idea what value it counted in the game. Was Glades improving and testing its defenses as part of a long-standing plan for world domination, or did more transpire in the heavens than Sam had believed? On the way home, he would have to make one more quick stop, at the Miami Excavation Project. If anyone knew what was going on, his old friend Areal Silvas did.

As he stepped up into *Whelp II*, Sam turned his head back toward Thorsel and grinned. "If you take over Key West, who'll clean Sudger's latrine?"

He watched as the hatch cut off view of Thorsel's empurpled face.

Listening a second to Gibb's quiet breaths, Sam thought of his dreams of tightrope walking. Every year the game becomes more complex. And deadly, he thought.

3

Gibb stood alone on the ship's upper deck, watching it approach a distant inlet, seen as a wide, rippling opening between giant, spreading trees. All about him the greenish blue water undulated and sparkled under an afternoon sun, lapping against the magic craft's sides. An azure sky exploded here and there with gold-lined puffs of cotton. He took a deep breath of salt air and trembled with joy.

He thought of the day before. Though the great lord had had every right to kill him for his stupid attempt at murder, he had been merciful. The city-lord reminded him of the red-bearded lord who had given the Peakers food in their harshest winter; they did not look at all alike, rather they both moved through the world with such clarity of purpose, with such commanding certainty. As the warm breeze caressed his bare chest, Gibb thought of love.

The Peaker chief, Onalsey, had cared for him, protecting him, feeding him when food was dear, keeping him warm during the mountain nights, taking pleasure from his body and giving it in return. Was this not love? Yet, Onalsey had three wives also. If something warms you, is it not a fire?

"Voice," Gibb spoke to the air, just loud enough to be heard over the squawks of great dingy-white sea birds hovering above.

"YES, GIBB."

"I have not seen the city-lord since his mercy toward me. Is he very angry?"

"KEEP ONE HAND ON THE RAIL, FOR YOU MAY BE DIZZY AT TIMES FROM THE DRUG USED TO STOP YOUR ATTEMPTED HIJACKING. I THINK SAM IS ANGRY WITH HIMSELF FOR NOT BETTER EXPLAINING THAT YOU WOULD BECOME A CITIZEN OF KEY WEST."

"This place!" Excitement welled inside him; his heart sped, and his skin flushed—a home!

"NO. THE ISLAND IS STILL TWO HUNDRED MILES SOUTH. WE ENTER THE MIAMI RIVER."

Gibb looked about the ship as it passed from choppy ocean into an area of calm between long arms of piled stones. As they moved into the river mouth, the water altered color from blue to pea-green to muddy-tan afloat with leaves and jumping things. Trees overhung the banks, and people moved among them. The ship appeared headed for a long wooden dock close ahead.

Sensuous nature returned Gibb's mind to thoughts of love, touching smooth bodies, and the lord's strangely timed kiss. "Does the city-lord have wives?"

He heard a low female chuckle. "SEVERAL MATES. ALL MALE, HOWEVER."

An image of his immediate competition, darkly handsome Brio, came to mind, was compared mentally with his own rather scrubby form, and Gibb lost the contest. Likely, only a new home would have to be enough for now.

A ringing came to Gibb from back toward the hatch where he had come up to look about. He turned too fast and his vision blurred and spun, then snapped back. The tall, snowy-haired city-lord had come on deck and walked toward him. He climbed the stairs to where Gibb stood, halted a few feet from him; and looked down with coal-black eyes and an unreadable expression on a smooth and lean tanned face.

Gibb disengaged from the man's gaze and looked at the

ribbed, gray-metal deck. "I'm sorry, lord."

"As well you should be! The blade started rusting before I could return it to the case. That dagger's twelve hundred years old—valuable!"

It took Gibb a second to realize that the city-lord was chastising him not for attempted murder, but rather for removing his knife from its holder! He looked back up into a beautiful smile, which he quickly returned.

The ship gently bumped against a massive wooden post. Lines of shiny metal snaked out from the craft and twined about it, snugging *Bitch* into place.

"Now, if you'll behave yourself, you can meet a very special man."

Gibb felt his face heat with a blush as he nodded, bubbling with excitement when the lord put an arm about him and led him to the side of the boat.

As he watched, a section of the ship's side altered shape and rolled out to meet a pier of gray wood planking. They stepped onto it and moved toward the shore, clunking all the way.

The air smelled of rich mud; insects buzzed and chittered to the heavens. They left the wooden pier and moved onto a light-dappled path, which ascended a low hill, between great trees with roots hanging from their limbs. Green-feathered birds squawked at them and took flight, opened wings revealing orange spots. They passed a young woman, who smiled. At the ridgetop, a view of flatness opened up before them. As far as Gibb could see there stretched a field of short grasses interrupted at times by sparkles of silver water. Here and there, well spaced, large mounds rose above the landscape. Some of these had been cleared down to white stone, while others housed gardens of moss and of thin-frond ferns tossing in the sea air.

Something scurried away from them, making a terrible racket among the dried leaves as it fled. They moved inland,

and the air took on a musty sourness from the presence of stagnant water.

"This used to be a city," the lord said to him as he waved an arm to indicate the field of mounds to either side of the path.

Gibb asked, "What happened to it?"

The man returned his arm to Gibb's shoulders and pulled him closer as they walked. He trembled again at the touch. "One summer over six hundred years ago three hurricanes, one after the other, ripped into the place. Leveled it!" His voice seemed to become more distant. "Nobody wanted to rebuild. The National Government of Florida didn't have the money, and businessmen knew the seas were slowly rising. What you see here was under twenty feet of water until three hundred years ago.

"Lot of people thought this site had been cursed by God. Remind me sometime, and I'll tell you the story of Key West and Miami's Preacher John."

Just then they walked around one especially large mound and into a massive excavation scene. A dozen or so tiny hills lay covered by small animals that dug out tufts of grass or carried away bites of dirt in their mouths. A high tower, loaded with equipment that shifted and sparkled in the afternoon sun, rose in the exact center of this field. The path led into the middle of the area and so Gibb got a closer look at the cat-sized creatures working about the place. Some had four legs, others six, some two hands, others only pinchers to pull at the grass.

As he watched, fascinated, and stopped in his tracts, one creature folded in on itself and changed shapes, then flowed apart and slowly became two creatures!

"Sam! Oh, sorry, my lord!"

The tall man had halted, with his hands on his hips, some ten feet on along the path. "Whale piss, Gibb! My name is 'Sam' and if you call me 'lord' in Key West, you'll embarrass the hell out of me! Those things," he pointed toward the one-become-two, "are digging machines designed with a fine touch for archaeological sites. They're Von Neumann machines—ah, they reproduce themselves."

Gibb followed Sam on toward the tower, but he couldn't keep his eyes off the busy creatures. They could not be machines; the city-lord was kidding him.

Before the tower's lower doorway stood a tall, wrinkled man with but a fringe of white hair left surrounding a shiny scalp. He greeted Sam with a hug, and Gibb could see the glistening of tears in the old man's eyes. This must be the city-lord's father, he thought.

"And who have you here, Samuel?"

The old man's attention and smile had turned to him.

"This is Gibb. We plucked him from the tender mercies of Charlotte's border police. Gibb, allow me to introduce Areal Silvas, a longtime business partner and friend—and amateur archaeologist."

He came to the boy and hugged him as well, but Gibb could feel the man shake—he was of an age long past when tribesmen wandered to the windswept peaks to die.

Silvas turned back to Sam. "You must come inside and see how much has been added to our model of Miami."

They entered the cool dimness out of the bright sun. When Gibb's eyes adjusted, he saw a large circular room walled in glass with its few pieces of furniture turned facing a central platform, a stage. Dancers! Gibb thought expectantly.

When they had taken a seat, the room lighting vanished completely and the stage took on a bluish glow, which extended into a fog that floated only above this one area in the room. He jumped. The stage filled with a collection of blue, green, and pink glass and metal shapes made from small tiles and connected by ribbons of shiny steel. A band of mirror twisted and turned its way along at the base of these objects.

"Smaller than I thought. Half the size of Glades," Sam commented.

Now, Gibb knew what he looked at: a picture of the city that had once existed here. The fine ribbons were roadways to and from great buildings. He felt his mouth hanging open and closed it. God's curse had destroyed much.

"Well, Samuel, you must remember how ancient these ruins are. And in any case no one had the know-how or funds to build really grand structures during the twenty-second century—this was pre-ceramsteel."

For several minutes no one spoke as they admired the city-picture, which turned and sometimes enlarged for better viewing. At last the scene returned to fog, and the room lights rose to a warm yellow.

"Things are changing, Samuel. I do not have much longer —nor do I want it! At least this missing link of Cuban heritage is returned to us. From this place, we regained our island homeland. This place must be remembered. You understand, Samuel?"

Gibb watched his rescuer nod, thoughts seemingly far away.

The aged man reached a trembling hand into a pocket of his loosely fitting coat and took out a small box. He handed it to Sam. "This is for Thomas. It is unlikely I can obtain more, however, Glades presses us. You understand, Samuel, that I cannot risk losing New Havana's supply of Lifestend. You do understand?"

Again Sam nodded, but his expression appeared stuck between sadness and anger. "Glades is winning control, isn't it, Areal?"

The old man let out a sigh. "Yes. Last month they forced Space Construction to sell their six largest orbital platforms. Soon, they'll have the gun loaded and aimed at our head. That age takes me, I am glad!"

"Areal, what can you tell me about the Titan rebellion?"

The old one was silent for a long moment, then he looked from Gibb to Sam and back again, at last saying, "The rebellion, it has spread. Also, it has continued much longer than anyone not privy to Solsys data knows—nearly ten years!"

With this, Sam shifted and sat up straight on the couch.

Areal Silvas continued: "Solsys sent out a fleet of some sixty armed spacecraft. They haven't been heard from in two years. Rumor says that space farther out than Mars is radio dead!" He shrugged and rubbed his hands together in short, jerky motions as if he were freezing.

"It's always nice to know that Glades has problems."

Silvas's voice dropped to a whisper that Gibb could barely hear. "I have my own hunch about what may be going on with those so-called rebels. That hunch I'll give you in a single name: Augustus Kittmore."

Gibb watched color drain from Sam's face.

"Who's Augustus Kittmore?" he asked, too curious to be silent any longer.

Sam's answer came out automatically, for he stared at blank wall across the room; his mind was elsewhere. "A man we both knew, a scientist and a builder."

"A man of great vision," Silvas whispered.

They stayed at the Miami camp long enough to sip cool rum drinks—which made Gibb dizzy—and to relive a round of memories that Gibb enjoyed adopting as his own. To the Peakers, story telling had been a major pastime. When at last they departed, the old man hugged Sam long and hard, tears again flowing off his wrinkled cheeks.

Along the trail back to the ship, Gibb, or perhaps the rum, asked, "He cried so when you left—was he once your lover?"

Sam turned his head and smiled. "More complex than that. Areal crossed into his hundred and fifteenth year last month—"

"Wow!"

"When he was a warm and squirmy boy of six, I held him on my knee and told him stories of lost cities."

Gibb halted. "City-lor—Sam, how old are *you*?"

"Little more than a hundred years older than Areal." Sam's eyes again became lost in thought, and he turned and resumed the trek back.

The thoughts—and now-obvious conclusions!—that came washing into Gibb's mind left him in awe: The city-lord Samuel Phoe was one in the same with the Old One of the Islands, the warrior hero in Chief Onalsey's tales, those whispered to him as they lay together late on winter nights.

Gibb thought, *I tried to kill a god*!

On their return along the boardwalk to *Bitch*, Sam Phoe's mind vibrated between thoughts of the dying Areal Silvas and the long dead Augustus Kittmore. How much time would pass before he joined them? He had begun to age; would it continue slowly, normally, or would he disintegrate the way his lover Thomas Sethy did? Sam felt cold inside.

Areal had suggested some connection between Kittmore and the rebellions in deep space, but Kittmore had been dead a hundred years! Still, he was glad that this hint of Auggy's involvement came after his meeting with Sudger. That bastard would have read a connection between them—though one as lovers, eons before. It would have been sticky.

Glancing at Gibb out of the corner of his eye, Sam noted that the boy kept looking at him and tripping on the planking. "What's wrong, Gibb?"

"Nothing! Lord Sam."

Sam shook his head and walked on toward the ship. As they came to the dock, he could see that *Bitch*'s secondary bay stood open, and she swallowed a duplicate to his omnicraft—*Whelp I* was home. He had a visitor. What, he wondered, couldn't wait till tomorrow morning?

Sounding a dull clank, they jumped onto *Bitch*'s deck, ascended two companionways and entered the unmanned upper bridge. Cool air gave Sam a shiver. He glanced at its curving wall of blinking instruments and controls, used only if something happened to the ship's cyberbrain. The elevator lay straight ahead; they entered. Down one deck, it opened into the comm room and lower bridge. With Gibb in his wake, Sam turned quickly out of the control area, passed through a set of air locks, and entered the ship's main salon into a strong odor of dry straw. The grass wall covering was still curing.

"Ah, Sam. There you are."

Cullji Lu slowly raised his hand in greeting, having removed it from fingering a mounted section of architrave from the US Supreme Court building. The thin and bearded yellow-cast face held a warm smile. He walked from the room's corner and took Sam's hand.

"You know," his voice sounded like the twang of a tightly strung banjo, "this is the first time I've been aboard your new ship. Impressive! All you need is a pipe organ—and you can change your name to Captain Nemo!"

Sam grinned, and Lu chuckled as *Bitch* chorded several deep organlike notes. He felt his mood buoy up, though he suspected it might not last past the reason for the vice mayor's visit.

After an early and light dinner of grilled salmon with fennel-cream sauce and even lighter conversation, the four humans aboard *Bitch* took crystal snifters of brandy and settled into the main salon's wicker chairs. Ten jokes and three stories into the evening, Lu caught Sam's eye and nodded toward the two young men.

"No point in secrecy, Lu. I'm always mumbling around Brio, and our newest citizen here," he winked at Gibb, "may as well hear some of the dirty politics of his hometown."

Lu exhaled a long breath. "Kenton White, taking his election to head the Assembly as a vote for his policies, has come out against you in a dozen places at once."

Sam's mind returned a picture of the blond and blue-eyed Kenton, smooth and muscular body stretched out on green sheets, wide boyish grin replying to Sam's old jokes, a deep and warm voice that made words sonic works of art. His hand had become sore; he looked down at the crinkled welts formed in it by trying to crush the wicker chair arm.

". . . and he's persuaded the Assembly to end government funding for Sugarloaf and Cudjoe."

He realized that act left him perhaps three weeks to find new money or reverse the Assembly's decision before the straight Excludeds on the north keys began to run out of building supplies—and hope. Sam had planned to take two years to make those people selfsufficient; White had cut him off.

"Whale piss!"

"It worsens, Sam."

He took a deep sniff of the warm Devas '87 that filled his glass, thinking of his dreams of tightrope walking, realizing now why those night visions made sense. The brandy's sharp and heady aroma steadied his nerves; he had begun to feel panic, and that was something those about him mustn't see.

"Remember the agreement you reached with Universal Products when Timmy Leos got caught using an automated drill in his shop?"

Sam allowed his mind a calming moment and listened to soft flutes, playing a piece by the Twenty-Fourth Century composer Lilliax. Timmy wasn't the only businessman in Key West who violated Corporate monopolies by moving beyond handmade goods; half the island's workers cheated in one way or the other. Timmy had gotten a fine, paid by Sam, and that had ended it.

"White's talked the Leos into appealing."

Sam bolted straight up out of his chair. "Shit! They'll have an audit team down on us! What is Kenton trying to do? I know he wants my ass out—but why damage his own city? His family's lived in Key West for eight hundred years!"

"Maybe that's why," Cullji Lu said softly.

Sam paused in his outrage and glanced at the two youths.

Gibb sat on the edge of his chair, wide-eyed; Brio eyed Gibb with a less than generous expression on his face. "The *why* is that Kenton White is arrogant, vain, and self-seeking! He wants his golden locks on a golden coin!"

Moving very slowly, Lu leaned back in his chair. "Sir, may I be frank?"

The man's formal tone washed Sam with a chill. He gave a grunt and nodded. His chair creaked and popped as he sat back down.

"I say this hoping not to draw your anger. Of late you have not made yourself available to defend your projects. And White has some good points. . . ."

The tips of Sam's ears began to heat up.

". . . and all three Houses of the Assembly are listening: The Conchs and the Middle House vote with White and many of the Lambdas do too! Why? No one in Key West but yourself and Hacker knows anything about foreign policy: the squabbles with Glades—'baiting the demon,' in White's words; this secret trade agreement over Timmy's drills; your buying up all the party drugs with city funds—"

"Whale piss and salmon shit! I buy up Easelax and dump it down the john. If I don't grab that zombie milk, it'll be sold in our stores. That crap's addictive and toxic! Do any of you have the least idea what dealing with the Corporates is like?"

When Sam's echoed yells died down, Lu whispered, "No, Sam, even your vice mayor has very little idea beyond what The Great Mother, as White names you, tells him."

Shaking slightly, Sam glared into Lu's slanted eyes. He inhaled deeply. Each generation does this, he thought, trying to put the words into perspective and lower his blood pressure. Lu, after all, was one of his most loyal supporters; and if *he* came to say these words, then matters moved far out of hand. "How bad is it, Lu?"

His friend visibly relaxed, but remained sitting upright in the chair. "The Assembly is in a foul mood. Unless tensions ease, they may force you to decide the full use of your Fundies."

And there it was.

The old question: Was Samuel Phoe an elected official, or was he a military dictator, having conquered the island town a hundred and eighty-seven years before? Was he kidding himself? Was he really a modern, if less grand, version of Augustus Caesar, who praised the return of the Roman Republic, but who came to crucial votes in the Senate accompanied by a cohort of the Praetorian Guard?

The salon tilted slightly, evidenced by a leaning of the wrought-iron chandelier centered in the room and hanging over a glass holograph table. *Bitch* was diving, likely avoiding choppier seas detected by her four outrider drones.

"I'm sorry, Lu. Too hot about this now. I'll think it over and—much as I detest the idea—meet with Kenton when we get home." (It annoyed Sam to no end that he couldn't stop calling White by his first name.) He changed subjects. "Where was Hacker when you left? He's been off-line for days."

Lu shrugged. "Haven't seen him, Sam. Oh, there is another minor problem. Secret police from Glades arrested a visitor yesterday, one Alexander of Titan . . ."

Major problem! thought Sam.

". . . but the Fundies broke him loose until I could speak with you. The man apparently has been spending all his time on Key West visiting other off-islanders and reviewing the city's historical records. Glades has refused to list a charge." Lu dug into the pocket of his blue dress jacket, took out a thin card, and stuck it into a slot in the holo table.

The 3-D image of a giant, red-bearded young man appeared instantly—a good-looking fellow in big trouble, but what could he do? Sudger had a hard-on for anyone from Titan.

"We'll have to let them have him—"

A sharp gasp from Gibb interrupted Sam's words. The boy jumped over to before him, kneeling and clutching at

Sam's hand. His words sounded frantic:

"I lied to you, Lord Sam! I lied about the silver coin! That man gave it to me. He saved my entire tribe. Please, don't let them kill him."

Sam began, "They probably just have questions for him—"

Gibb squeezed Sam's hand tighter. "Please, lord, my life for his—anything you want from me!"

Bitch intervened. "SHALL I CONTACT CAPTAIN FORDAC, SAM?"

From *Bitch*, that was a strong hint of which direction correctness lay. He sighed and affirmed.

A minute passed, then the Titanian's image vanished in a dance of blue sparks. A man dressed in a long white robe appeared; only fierce blue eyes defined a human, for cloth head-covering was wrapped across his lower face.

The Captain of the Fundy Guard raised his right hand in salute. "Hail, Samuel!"

"How are your people, Uriel?"

"God punishes us."

Fordac's response was pure ritual. Still, the statement always grated at Sam, for the Fundies believed that their God forced them to guard and police Sodom as punishment for the sin of once revealing the tenets of their religion to unbelievers. He couldn't imagine this himself, for at the time he rescued the Fundies from the destruction of World City-State that place's dominant religious sect had imprisoned them, calling the group "the Dumb" because they were so intensely antievangelical.

Did he dare defy Glades so soon after Sudger's warning? There had been a strong hint in Areal Silvas's tone that Key West might not be able to count on New Havana's support if matters once again came to a showdown. He thought of Kenton White's accusations over foreign policy, realizing suddenly how few on the island knew that there had been a major naval confrontation between Glades and New Havana over the rights to Key West in 2709.

Sam looked down into Gibb's saucerlike black eyes. What the hell! he thought. "Uriel, guard this Alexander of Titan. And toss those Glades agents off the island. Quite literally, if you like!"

"Hail, Samuel." The robed man's image vanished from atop the table.

Sam glanced down at Gibb. "Happy?"

The boy nodded. Tears ran down his cheeks from sparkling, wet eyes. Sam looked up and over to where Brio sat. The dark youth smiled, but not fast enough. A deep frown had lined his face a split second before.

Sam had seen his guests aboard *Bitch* off to bed, but he himself went forward to the comm room to renew his efforts at contacting Hacker. Needing some way to sift through the mountain of disinformation put out by World-News, and to raid data bases, he had purchased one of the most advanced free-roaming robots he could find. Now, apparently, it had roamed away.

His efforts proved as ineffective as *Bitch*'s. Hacker, bought when he had more money, was one of Auggy Kittmore's designs; if the cyberbrain was damaged, Sam could afford neither repair nor replacement.

"Whale piss!" He pounded the comm console.

A black curtain began to drop over Sam's spirit as he crossed the salon, heading toward his cabin and more dreams of hapless tightrope walking. He thought again of a forced meeting with Kenton White, and a knot formed in his throat. Right after their breakup, he had convinced himself that he never wanted to see Kenton again, and had nearly effected this by isolating himself in Whitehead Palace. Now, he realized there was still a bond between them. But what kind of bond? Would Sam be forced to play Arthur to White's Modred?

Key West, 2720 A.D.

As the door to his cabin slid open, dim yellow lighting came up softly to coat with its mellow glow the oak paneling and wide bed across the room. The bed wasn't empty!

Blinking from the light, just reawakening, Gibb rolled onto his back and turned those enormous black eyes on him. The youth smiled, then placed hands on thighs and lifted olive-tan legs up into the air, bent his knees, and exposed buttocks and the center of his sexual life.

Tribal ways lacked subtlety, Sam realized, but they were effective: A "no, thank you" couldn't get past a numb tongue. Despite two hundred years of practice at sex, he trembled. The iron rod between his legs would no longer accept rationalizings about the danger of affairs with island boys—shades of Kenton White! No, the rod wanted action or it would turn on Sam and run him through the bowels.

Was this what the boy had meant by "I'll do anything" when the red-haired savior of his erstwhile tribe had been in danger? Who cares?—on with it! the rod demanded.

Sam walked over to the bed. He sat on the edge, placing one hand on the silky blue sheets and the other on Gibb's chest. The boy's skin felt warm and soft as the finest leather. His fingers roamed to an erect nipple the color of freshly turned earth. He kneaded it. Gibb moaned.

Sam leaned over close to his face. "May I start up here?"

He kissed the full, cool lips. And as Gibb lowered his legs and wrapped him with his arms, Sam could see the bobbing shadow of the boy's erection playing across his belly. Not entirely obligation, Sam thought.

The scent of Sam's favorite orange cologne wafted up to him from Gibb's excited warmth. Only *Bitch* could have told him where to find that—his crew conspired against him!

Stop thinking! yelled the rod.

At some point, near four in the morning, they halted exploits and exploration by mutual, unspoken consent. Sam felt physically drained and weak, but, more importantly, mentally renewed. When he was about to drift off into what was left of sleeping time, Gibb made a demand:

"Tell me a story."

"Story?" *The boy isn't that young,* thought Sam.

"Sure. After Onalsey made love to me—if he didn't have to please a wife later—he always told me a story before we went to sleep. Some were about you!"

Sam thought: *Oh, no.*

"I know," the boy bubbled, "tell me about Key West and Priest John!"

"Preacher John." Sam resigned himself to no sleep. He pulled the youth closer to him. "It's a founding myth for Key West as it is today, though this all happened way back in twenty-one sixteen, six hundred years ago."

Gibb snuggled closer still. Sam wondered how the boy would take parting from him when they reached the island, for part they must.

"It was a time of confusion and lost hope, a time of dying for long-held ideas. The great government that had held half a continent of people together as one was gone. In its place the smaller governments—once called 'states'—held on to order, but weakly. Fear and doubt ruled men's hearts.

"Miami, the site we just left, had been hit harder than most. For a hundred years the exiled Cubans living there had transformed its soul to their Latin beat. But they were gone, returned to their home island when the government known as the Great Bear toppled to ruin and could no longer support its client state in Cuba. So, you see, Miami had lost its soul. It reveled in violence and hate.

"Into this came Preacher John." He turned his head to see if Gibb had dropped off to sleep yet. No such luck; the boy looked at him wide-eyed.

"Preacher John preached hate. He needed a target and picked the nearby colony of gays who had resided in Key West for many years. These sodomites, he said, had brought the destruction of their beloved country—"

"The Great Bear?"

"No, no. The one that had existed here, the Great Eagle. He preached his message week after week, beginning in the spring of that year. Few paid attention, his was not a new line.

"On Key West, the Conchs did listen. Not so much because men loving men bothered them—they had lived with worse, and the gay population was old hat. They listened because thousands of new gays poured onto the island each year as local governments across the continent became repressive to anyone who differed from the common. The Conchs were being pushed off their island.

"Support in Key West didn't help fill Preacher John's coffers in Miami. An idea came to the man. The first Sunday in July he announced that God would destroy Key West that very year, just as He had leveled Sodom. A great hurricane, Preacher John said, would scrape away all evil in that place.

"Now this got him attention!

"The news organizations of the time began attending his sermons. With each preaching, John became bolder, at last naming a date—September tenth—when the great storm would come. The newsmen snickered. The Conchs on Key West were not amused. Preacher John warned them to leave Sodom.

"Everyone stopped laughing at John when, on the night of September seventh, a tiny tropical depression suddenly began strengthening. It churned about southwest of Key West, in the Gulf of Mexico. By the eighth, the storm, called Michael by Preacher John, had winds of a hundred and twenty miles an hour—"

"That would scour an island?"

"And then some. But by early morning on the tenth, no weather instrument of the day could measure the storm's speed of rotation without burning out. The sky all about Key West turned the color of a bruise, waterspouts surrounded the island. Michael moved to the east and sat, churning and flooding Key West with skys full of rain. Waves ate the docks and beaches. Storm tides had closed, then bitten away the only route north, off the island.

"Most of the gays who were the least religious, and many who were not, filled a small chapel the gay community had built for itself. They came to pray. Many Conch families saw where these unwanted citizens went on a morning when safety demanded anyone with good sense take deep shelter. A handful of these families came out into the lightning-filled blackness and joined the gays—"

"All in the small chapel?"

"Yes. So tightly pressed together that no one could move, or survive when the storm hit.

"Preacher John, meanwhile, was having a field day. The world press followed his every pronouncement as if he were truly the direct voice of God. Money rolled in even as this unfolded. He was about to become the holy man of the century; he would unite all the God-fearing people in America. Journalists speculated that he might reunite their fractured nation.

"God, it seems had other ideas about Preacher John. Michael had been born in the Gulf, best of all birthplaces for such storms, had moved off the coast of Key West—but then began to travel northward, always just off the various keys. It didn't stop until it reached Miami. There it halted and spun, a black presence twenty miles off the coast, hurling a wall of rain at the city.

"People fled Miami. For good reason. Michael came ashore like an avenging demon from hell that had turned on its master, ripping at Miami for six days, grinding the city.

"And in case someone had missed the point, when Michael had become a warm breeze, two more storms formed. They too hit the city that summer. No one ever rebuilt the place, for the oceans were rising even then."

Gibb stirred beside him. "Wow. What happened to Preacher John?"

"Swept away by Michael." Actually, as Sam recalled, Preacher John had fled the city early and resumed selling used farm machinery in Clewiston.

Not being fond of the divine intervention theory, Sam had always believed that some of the world-class Corporates of the day had used early weather-modification technology to dampen religious fanaticism, which they perceived as bad for business. Maybe. Having lived a hundred years beyond any reasonable explanation, Sam was no longer sure what he believed.

"Was that enough story for you?" he asked Gibb.

The boy bobbed his head up and down. "The Conchs and the gays became friends?"

"Yes, but that took another two hundred years after the hate stopped. Now, you tell me a story. About silver coins and red-bearded men."

Gibb stirred beside him and sat up against the leather-padded headboard. Glancing sideways, Sam observed a wave of pain contort Gibb's face for a second and fill his eyes with tears. The youth remembered his tribe.

"Summer before last was hard for the Peakers. Hunting had been thin. Heavy rains rotted the potatoes we had planted and caused berries to drop from the bushes before they ripened. Not just us. All the mountin tribes lacked enough food to see them through the snows and ice. Onalsey feared that the tribes would fight again, raiding one another's supplies, taking prisoners to eat when other foods ran out. I was afraid.

"When the red and orange leaves began to fall and cold had settled in, word passed by runner among the tribes that some men with the dress of great city-lords gave out strange food. This they did in a high valley three day's march from where we camped. Onalsey took ten men, and me. I was his favorite. The chief feared a trap, for the cities lately had begun attacks against the mountain tribes. Yet when we arrived, half frozen from the chill and high winds of the place, all was as the runners had said.

"Six men and two women waited there with large crates of food. The food appeared odd. It was thin, transparent sheets in various colors. At first Onalsey would not taste it. But by the time we had reached this peak, my stomach groaned; I stepped forward, hand out. The man with the red beard grinned at me and offered a small piece of a yellow sheet. It was ripe melon! Everyone burst out laughing, I think it must have been the look on my face."

Sam asked, "Did these people say why they gave out the food or where they came from?"

"Onalsey talked to them for some time before we left with our food, but he never told me that they said to him, except . . . that night, in his sleep, Onalsey kept mumbling something—'Starcastle.'

"The red-bearded man gave our chief a bag of silver coins to buy other goods from the traders. Mine, the leader gave to me personally. There is no more story."

"Come on! Let's wash up before trying to get an hour's sleep," Sam said as he patted Gibb's stomach and climbed out of the slippery satin sheets.

The ultrasonic shower, Sam thought, might get my brain working!

Without his logic in top form, he could never make sense of Gibb's tale. Why would off-worlders come here to feed ragtag tribes of Excludeds? Were they rebels plotting some sabotage against the Corporates or city-states? Possible. In which case, his actions to protect their leader would place him and Key West in extreme danger.

Inside the shower, clouds of dancing and vibrating mist enveloped them. Sam felt its soothing tingle in every muscle fiber. Curly hair wet and smoothed back, body glistening from the water spray, Gibb came to him, snaking firm yet soft arms about his waist and leaning his head against Sam's chest.

"Make love to me!" the youth ordered.

The Colonel had taught Sam that a good soldier never disobeys an order.

4

Gibb awakened to the city-lord's gentle snoring. He did not know what time it was, but the same clock that woke him from a bed of leaves had forced his eyes open here. It was nearly dawn. Taking a second to rub his fingers against the lord's snowy hair, he then slipped from bed, pulled on some soft pants and a stiff jacket that the Voice had given him, and returned to his chamber. He knew the way on deck. See that first glimmer of his new home, he must.

The hall outside was empty—no sign of the youth called Brio, who made Gibb apprehensive. Moving along the hall, he entered the widened area where the twisting stairs turned upward to the ship's outside deck. Clanging up and around these, Gibb came to the sealed round portal. It remained closed.

"WE ARE UNDER THIRTY FEET OF WATER, GIBB," the ship's voice said.

"Oh. I wanted to see Key West the minute it came into view. It's my new home!"

The ship tilted slightly, forcing his back against the hard railing. He remained there, not returning downward. In about a minute, the hatch above him expelled a loud hiss and slid aside. A sticky spray shot down at him, soaking his clothing; a salty odor sent a surge of elation through Gibb's body.

He scrambled up the ladder and onto a deck still glistening with seawater running back into the ocean. A chilly breeze made him regret having got soaked.

The easterly sky was alight with a heavy gray, which served as background for a wan section of moon and a bright morning star. The sea held the color of new iron, sparkling along a strip where the crescent shone down. Nowhere about the ship could Gibb see land.

As he stood there, the sky became blue-gray and misty, looking as if a fog hung farther out to sea. These became gray clouds lined in dirty pink. He turned his back on the east and looked west. In the pearly light he could now distinguish dark green shapes—islands. The ship slipped past these too rapidly for him to detect any structures on them. Yet, an increase of rosy light began to reveal the islands as covered with the same giant limb-rooted trees he saw when they had visited Miami the day before.

Gibb heard the clangor of footsteps on metal and spun about. The tall, yellow-skinned man walked toward him. He halted, pointing a slender finger toward the growing light. "'At first there was pink promise, which faded to gray, as if the sun would grant us light, but did not consider the day's worth sufficient to appear....' Wish those were my words. One of Sam's lovers, Tom Sethy, wrote it. Sometimes competing weather fronts stall out each other, and we suffer a foggy mist off the coast."

The man's twanging voice abraded Gibb's nerves, but a warm smile soothed the effect. "The ship's voice told me that Lord Sam has many lovers. Does he often take new ones?"

Chuckling, the man replied, "If you're interested in our Samuel, well, the line goes around the block. These days he seldom even makes love to fellow islanders, preferring to seduce tourists and odd visitors. He has his reasons, I suppose."

An orange ball appeared to the east, and the wind picked up, this time much warmer.

Rounding one of the vegetation-covered islands, the ship

passed before a flourishing colony: small huts and wood fires streaming smoke into the pink sky. Wooden sailing boats filled the water out from a rounded harbor.

"Key West!" Gibb shouted.

"Good Lord, no! That's Cudjoe Key, one of the Excludeds' camps Sam set up."

The sound of people yelling crossed the water to them, echoing like someone shouting from the bottom of a barrel. Cullji Lu tapped Gibb's shoulder and pointed toward the ship's highest mast. A thick cylinder there had opened and a banner unfurled. The gentle breeze fluttered it open enough for him to make out the design: A seashell atop a radiant sun on a background of blue composed half the flag, while the remainder was a field of pink covered by gold shapes looking like the letter "y" upside down.

Many of the small craft in the water began to glide up, dwarfed by the hundred and seventy foot city-lord's metal ship. Those in the tiny boats cheered and waved greetings, some bent over double in a bow, as *Bitch in Heat* silently slipped by them. Gibb waved.

"Pharaoh's barge," Lu mumbled under his breath.

Shortly, a second island appeared, this one also covered by small structures and surrounded by waiting boats.

"Were they awaiting us?" Gibb asked.

"No. Setting out fishing when we happened by." Lu pointed southeast at a set of twin towers rising on the gray-blue horizon. "A touring ship."

"That's a boat!" It appeared like part of some city. Gibb had seen nothing so large since he had last looked upon the buildings of Charlotte when he was twelve.

"They carry some ten thousand people, travel all over the world. Bring a lot of business to our little island." Again he pointed, this time to a pair of smaller ships, themselves immense, one ahead and one behind the giant ship.

"Destroyers."

Suddenly, the light about them dimmed by half.

"*Bitch*'s mirror shield went up," Lu commented, just before Gibb panicked.

A voice came from behind him; Gibb jumped when a hand gently squeezed the back of his neck, sending a tingle up and down his spine: "Now, *Bitch*, don't go shooting at our paying customers!"

He turned and looked into Sam Phoe's face. The man's eyes were fixed on a point over Gibb's shoulder. The boy turned about and saw Key West.

From this distance the island looked like a fortress in the desert. Rather than beginning at beach level, the city's gray-white and umber buildings—true colors muted by a thin fog—rose from atop a continuous white wall that ended well above the sea and shoreline.

"Years ago—people here raised the island forty foot above sea level to prevent flooding. They dug up several adjoining keys for their rock and sand," said Lu. "In fact, water did eventually come three-quarters up those walls. Then went back down. We have our beaches back, now."

As they moved closer, the wall lost its even appearance, becoming more clearly something hurriedly constructed by filling in between old structures, which still stuck out from the wall like fossils from sandstone. Here and there at beach level stood clusters of tall palms. Above the wall, groves of trees in every shade of green surrounded white, blue, and pink buildings. Even more colorful awnings eyebrowed their windows and doorways.

A deep bass horn sounded from the distant touring ship.

"*THEY WILL STAND DOWN TILL WE DOCK, SAM,*" the ship said, against the moan of a rising wind. *Bitch* was rocking slightly.

"No need. We'll slip into my harbor—"

Lu interrupted him. "Now, Sam, you know you're part of the show."

"Whale piss!"

A puff of smoke appeared from atop a reddish outjutting of the white wall. A boom made Gibb jump. This repeated one after the other until the sea rolled with thunderlike noise.

Lu tapped Gibb's shoulder, pointing toward a golden beach and a wide set of stairs that ascended to an opening in the wall. Through the opening he saw parks and terraced buildings gleaming red from sunshine on polished stone. Yellow- and white-striped awnings fluttered over every window, reminding Gibb of a great swarm of spring butterflies.

"Casa Marina Hotel. Actually more expensive than Sam's hotel," said Lu as he looked sideways at the mayor and grinned.

His gaze darting along the city, trying to take it all in, Gibb noted a promontory along the wall beside a tall and wide windowless structure of purest white. On the promontory, dozens —no hundreds!—of colorfully dressed people stood, waving and shouting out greetings that failed to carry across the water to them. *Bitch* turned to round the end of the key and Gibb glimpsed the grandest building he could ever remember seeing.

It stood above a section of wall far higher than that about the rest of the Key West. A multilevel forest stepped its way up to the highest point, where the building itself stood. Two layers of sparkling white arches hundreds of feet long supported a steep roof of gray tile. Purple awnings shaded the lower arches.

"Narlo's been at it again!" hissed Sam. "When I left, those awnings were blue!"

Lu whispered in Gibb's ear as if trying not to draw the mayor's wrath. "Whitehead Palace." He nodded toward the vast structure.

Their ship rounded the point and moved farther out to sea, bypassing a black jetty of sharply pointed rocks that stabbed half a mile out into the ocean. This end of Key West looked much the same: high wall crowned by gardens and buildings. How many people, he wondered, lived here that they built so densely?

Entering the harbor, gently rocking in its slight swell, *Bitch* snugged up to the central dock, which jutted far out into the water. Gibb could discern a broad stone wharf with expansive stairs leading upward onto a plaza between two immense buildings. More, but narrower, steps ascended to a wide street that angled sharply off from the plaza below it. People, yelling and waving, lined the stairs clear up into the street—thousands of people! More people than Gibb had ever seen in one place!

"Sam's hotel, the Da Vinci, on the left, Hotel Walt Whitman on the right," said Lu, serving as self-appointed tour guide.

"Whale piss! Look at them. You'd think I was some victorious general returning from the front, not coming home from sucking ass in Albany!"

Gibb's gaze settled on the rows of white-clad men standing on the wharf. They were armed soldiers, hundreds of them, and they made him nervous.

A resounding shout arose from these men: "Hail, Samuel!"

Horns blared and a band farther along the wharf struck up the same tune Gibb remembered greeting the advent or departure of the President of Charlotte.

Sam waved to the people off in the distance, and spoke to Brio, who had come on deck unnoticed by Gibb. "Find out who's been assigned to Gibb here. Take the boy to him." He moved off the ship, but when Gibb went to follow, the young aide dug a grip into his arm.

"You're going a different way, kid."

They debarked from *Bitch in Heat* by a rear gangway and walked back seaward along the stone dock until they reached a railinged opening leading below. Their steps echoed hollowly inside the tunnel they entered. The place held a dank chill and an odor of fish; its lighting was dim and green.

"Come on, guys! You've got business," said Brio, talking to an inset metal door.

Gibb started at a vibrating hum. The metal door slid upward into the ceiling; a small cart with padded seats rolled out to them and stopped. The dark-skinned youth pointed that he should get on, while himself taking a seat and speaking to the machine: "Exit two."

The cart shot down the tunnel so fast that Gibb felt a cold wind on his face. At one point they passed a dozen well-loaded carts going the opposite direction; two men rode with these, and Brio waved at one.

"Any luck, Brio?" the fellow shouted. But Brio shook his head and scowled as they roared by.

They shot out into a wider and better lighted hall with narrower branches at right angles, spaced every hundred feet or so. Rather than gray concrete, the walls here sported brightly colored paintings of plants and of animals that Gibb doubted could really exist (one spotted creature was drawn with a neck as long as its legs!). Potted vines hung from wall brackets. The cart slowed.

Gibb asked, "Do people live down here?"

"Yeah, some. Sam doesn't like it, but there are nearly a hundred thousand citizens now—have ta go somewhere. Mostly, new arrivals, or guys with an aversion to work, live in the Pits. We're under Duval Street, main drag through the upper city. Two levels of factories and workshops are below us."

The cart made a fast turn, which nearly spilled an unaware Gibb out onto the roadway, and sped up a ramp. The machine came to a stop in a circular pit, roofed above by a green translucent dome supported by elaborate wrought-iron grillwork. Railinged stairways, with scrolled iron matching the grillwork above, curved upward along the wall.

They left the cart, which rolled away back into the tunnel; its echo sounded like angry bees. Brio led their way up into the light. As they emerged, a warm morning breeze tugged at Gibb's shirt; it carried the fragrance of more sweet-smelling blooms than his nose could define.

The pavilion, which covered the underground entrance, stood at one corner of two wide streets. Turning his head in a

Key West, 2720 A.D.

full circle, Gibb got the impression that these streets and the buildings lining them were sunk below other parts of the city. If he didn't hold his gaze down to street level, it tended to wander to the taller and newer-appearing structures that walled in this area.

Brio noticed him looking at these. "That's the rear of the big dockside hotels."

He dropped his attention to the lower wood and brick structures lining the streets. Never had Gibb seen buildings like these. They were ancient, and no two possessed the same design. Wooden porches and picket fences provided a common element with nearly unlimited variation. Wall-climbing vines and dense shrubs hid many structure partly or entirely from his view. Curving, white-gravel paths led off between buildings toward other homes or shops behind.

Crowds of brightly dressed people filled the wider tile-paved street to his right so densely that they flowed like water around the row of giant, spreading and blooming trees planted in the center—huge scarlet umbrellas.

"Come on! Let's go somewhere we can get breakfast, and I can use a terminal. Gotta find out where you belong." Brio pulled on Gibb's shirt, then headed down the lesser street away from the crowd.

The columned fronts of structures along the route stood open—making the lower floors one giant porch—displaying goods for sale: boxed and bagged foods, vast urns of flowers, dolls and manikins, glassware, carved and plain seashells. All went by Gibb's eyes: a blur as he attempted to keep up with Brio.

At last the young man halted before a gate and trellis; purple-flowered vines enveloped both. He appeared to think about something for a moment, then swung open the gate and ushered Gibb into a deeply shaded courtyard. Two dozen tables, covered with bright green cloths, surrounded a tinkling fountain. Gibb had gotten used to food rising out of tables, but these did not appear equipped for such. Another party, three men and a woman, sat in animated conversation, sipping drinks in the near corner.

"Perch here a minute." Brio strutted off toward an open doorway opposite the entry gate.

Gibb sat. Tingling with excitement, he gazed about in wonder—that these islanders could organize their lives to include such beauty and also leave people free to be who they wanted to be! Charlotte, vaguely remembered, had been monumental; and, even with some areas of restored old city, flashed in his memory as cold and rejecting.

Two young men about Gibb's age entered through the gate. One, tall and blond, kept nibbling at the ear of his freckly, red-headed friend; for them the rest of the world was empty. They took a table in a far corner under a striped umbrella. Gibb ached at the sight, wishing Kao were alive to be here, to see this, to nibble on his ear.

Brio returned, followed by a black-haired man with a pasty face who held two glasses on a small tray. Brio screeched a chair against the tile flooring as he took a seat. The waiter smiled broadly, set down the drinks, and left.

"Have to eat later. Not serving yet. Drink up!" said Brio as he poked at a weakly glowing translucent tile he had set on the table. Amazed, Gibb watched tiny symbols and diagrams appear on the tile in response to Brio's stroking.

Gibb took a deep swallow from the glass. Fire shot up his nose. He began choking.

"Sip, kid! Its hot buttered rum, not water. Oh, before I forget. These are yours, from Mayor Phoe." He dug into a pocket of his pants and brought out a stack of white metal coins. He clunked them on the table before Gibb, then took one back, "And thanks for the drink."

Gibb reached and took them, five in all now, looking at the seashell raised on the surface of the top coin. "What are they for?"

"Money, kid. A fair amount of it too—a hundred and twenty bucks! That'd keep me in good times all year. Wish I got paid so well for one screw. Ha, you'll be a candidate for Queens' Fraternity!"

Gibb didn't think that was why Lord Sam gave him the coins. "It's not for—!"

"None of my business! Look, this thing," he pointed at the glowing tile, "says you're assigned to Harsho Jones, of the Middle House. Never met him, but there ain't nobody unimportant in the Middle House. What happens is this: You get assigned to a sponsor—to give you a home, find you work—for your first year on Key West. When you've passed the twelve-month mark, you apply to a fraternity you like. To us gay men, a frat is like a big family—I'm a Walt myself. I mean my name may be Brio Dirrenni, but my legal last name on this island is 'Walt.' Follow me?"

Not sure he did, Gibb still nodded. His head was spinning slightly from the strong drink. "Middle House is a frat, right?"

"Wrong. Look. On this island, we got tourists, who spend money to keep us going—they're guests, and they can't stay more than a month. We got straight Excludeds that the Old Man keeps on Sugarloaf and Cudjoe; they need a visa to come here. We got Conchs, the old straight families who've lived on Key West for hundreds of years. They own most of the island. We got gays, who come here from all over the world—myself, I'm from Rome—and make up two-thirds of the population. Okay, kid. Who'd I leave out?" The youth's thick and connecting eyebrows rose expectantly.

Gibb giggled, he wasn't sure why. "Gay Conchs."

"Wow! You ain't as dumb as you look! On target—the Middle House. This Harsho Jones you've been assigned to is a gay Conch."

The same waiter returned with a second drink. When Gibb started to turn it away, Brio tapped his hand and whispered a "no." After the waiter left, he said, "The second one is a gift from the Palms, the frat that runs this place. Very bad form to refuse. Drink up!"

Giggling again, Gibb swallowed half the warm liquid in the glass; he was beginning to like the way it made his body feel—he floated! He felt happier. Rum seemed not to affect Brio, for the youth didn't even smile.

"You wanta be a part of Key West?"

Gibb swallowed hard. "More than anything."

This time Brio smiled broadly. "Well, nobody here's gonna say two words to ya unless you know the password."

"What's that?"

He shook his head. "The gays on this island want to know if a guy's got guts or not. You notice the white-uniformed guards at the pier?" Gibb nodded; he still had a chill from seeing them. "They're called 'Fundies.' What you gotta do is go up to one o' them and do this."

Brio scooted over to Gibb and grabbed him in the crotch, so hard that he winced. "Ouch! Do that in the tribes and a guy could get killed!"

"Yeah, maybe. But how many times you get screwed in the forest—men's men! And in any case this is gay Key West, not some mountaintop out in nowhere. Look, I'm just lettin' you in on something it takes new guys months to find out on their own. You grope a Fundy—maybe he decks you, but you'll still get the password. And then people'll let you inta things. Got it?"

"I guess. Seems awe . . . ful rude."

Brio grinned at him. "A message on the data plate says I gotta go over to my frat house. You find a Fundy to feel up, and I'll meet you back here for lunch."

Before Gibb could sort out a reply, Brio was gone. He sat alone at the table. A few minutes later he rose, stumbled over the extra chair, and walked with heavy feet across the patio to its far corner. He stopped before the table occupied by the two young men who had entered after them. They looked up at him, but their faces weren't in focus.

"You two lobbersss?" he mumbled; his tongue felt thick.

"Get lost!" one of them snapped at him.

Anxiety overcame Gibb. He ran for the gate, tripping once and bruising his knee. Outside on the street, his head cleared slightly. Now he realized what Brio had meant: no password, no talk! Rejection! Rejection from the city he desperately wanted to love and have love him in return. He still felt dizzy, like his head might spin off his neck.

Just then one of the white-uniformed Fundies walked by; he was a giant, more muscled that any man Gibb had ever seen. He could not see his face, for only fierce blue eyes showed above a wrap of his towering cloth headdress. He began to follow the soldier when a thought came to him: He didn't have to risk groping the biggest Fundy in Key West. He would look for a smaller one.

He wandered toward the tree-lined main street and out among the throngs. As Gibb staggered in a direction he guessed to be away from the docks where he had arrived, scenes of buildings and people swam about before him and blurred together. Combined voices became a high-pitched roar. Only the jar in his legs told him he moved rather than that the world floating by him.

A breeze delivered the scent of food, which brought to Gibb a wave of nausea. He stopped and held his nose to prevent vomiting on those about him. Hiccups produced a sour taste in his mouth. At last he gave up, stepped between a pair of red-brick storefronts, and poured his guts out in an alley.

Afterward, deep breaths cleared his head. Feelings of joy and elation returned. He would simply have to find a Fundy and get on with things. After the point where Duval Street crossed Truman Avenue, a colonnade began and ran for several blocks. The other side of its columns a vast park of shade-covered pink gravel paths and connecting ponds stretched out until it met terra cotta roofed buildings in the distance. First taking a deep breath of the place's blooms, Gibb turned away. He bumped into a white-clad Fundy. The man was twice his size; Gibb mumbled an apology and walked on.

Quick movement again made his head spin, but when vision cleared, Gibb saw a building he recognized. Directly across Duval Street from the park towered a block-sized structure of dull white finish, lacking any exterior window or opening. He remembered sailing past it on the way around to the dock; it had come just before *Bitch* had passed beneath the high ground Lu had called Whitehead Palace. As he watched, a section of stone wall moved inward, revealing a shadowed opening. Out walked a dozen Fundies. Now, Gibb knew what the building was: their fortress, below and protecting Lord Sam's great home.

Gibb's attention jumped to one member of the emerging group who drew off from the others and walked toward a small plaza at the end of the street. This soldier was smaller than him. At least the man might not be able to break every bone in Gibb's body if a grope infuriated him.

Following the soldier into the nearly deserted plaza, Gibb realized that this space was the overlook he had seen from the ocean side. A glinting, bronze statue rested atop a column of polished red stone at the center of the space, and his quarry halted before it. The man bowed his head, and stood there beside the column.

Crossing the space between them as quietly as years of stalking in the forest would allow, Gibb came up to the man, took a deep breath, and grabbed him between the legs.

Fiery green eyes looked into his for a second. The man shifted position. Gibb felt the earth fall away as hard stone thumped against his back and knocked the breath out of him. He tried to shift, but found he couldn't move anything other than his eyes. The soldier had one hand pinching Gibb's neck muscles, sending spikes of pain down his spine, while the other poised like an axe blade above his throat. He looked for fury in those green eyes, but saw only flowing tears. Had he hurt the man? Not likely; he hadn't found much to hurt.

With the high voice of a teenage boy, the soldier spoke to him: "What fraternity gets your body?"

5

Only one or two boos had disturbed Sam's progress from the docks to Whitehead, those likely Kenton White's people. But it wasn't the ones who yelled their dissatisfaction that bothered him; the parade route had been lined mostly by tourists. Along Duval Street, popular disaffection had been a suspicion; at the plazas before the Assembly Building he could taste its presence. Only half of the three hundred Assemblymen were present—of course, Kenton White was missing—and those who attended didn't smile much. How could morale go so far downhill in a month? he wondered.

Declining a cart in order to stretch his legs after so many days at sea, Sam walked up the gravel road to Whitehead. Uriel Fordac, Captain of the Fundy Guard, strode beside him. Overhead in the twin rows of date palms lining the route, wild parrots screeched at them, appearing as flashes of green and orange in the corner of his eye. Most of the hill lay covered by citrus trees. Their sweet fragrance became so potent that Sam welcomed the salty wind as they reached the higher ground before the palace.

"There is dissension in the city," Sam said, looking sideways at the chunky man dressed in white robes and wrapped headdress.

"Something is in the wind, Samuel."

"The stink of Kenton White's rhetoric!"

The Captain grunted. "Not that alone. Our prophet sees God's hand in what happens here—great change is near."

Your prophets see the hand of God in everything, thought Sam. But even a man as urbane as Areal Silvas had talked of change as if this time it should be spelled with a capital "C." Perhaps even he sensed it: What other explanation for his persistent dreams of tightrope walking? He knew one thing for certain: Key West was a rare and delicate environment existing this long only because the rest of humanity lived in fortified stagnation.

For Key West, change would be fatal.

As they approached the palace's platform terrace, the main doors of the building, set back inside high coral-stone arches, swung open and a dozen young men dressed in white duck pants and turquoise jackets ran out and down to line the stairs. The lead youth, with a gold collar on his coat, stopped before Sam.

"Welcome home, sir!"

Leaving Uriel Fordac on the landing, patting the majordomo on the shoulder, he smiled and winked his way up the wide steps, moved across the platform, and entered Whitehead Palace through its thirty-foot-high bronze doors. The minute he walked into the dimly lighted and echoing oval foyer he smelled it—the scent of new furnishings!

Ears beginning to burn, Sam stormed into the reception hall. Against every muraled wall rested a row of ornate gold and blue *fauteuil* awaiting royal bottoms. New. Expensive! The room's mosaic floor lay mostly hidden beneath an inch-thick cream and aqua rug—these were sold by the square inch and there was an acre of it in the hall! Each quadrant of the ceiling sported a new crystal chandelier descending from great folds of gold brocade. Sam was afraid to check any more rooms.

"Narlo!" he yelled. The sound echoed for several seconds.

The young butler approached, wearing a fearful expression. "Mister Adamms is with Mister Tom, sir."

He thinks he'll be safe with Tom! thought Sam, as he stormed back into the foyer and down a front hallway toward the west residential wing. Even here, he noted, new carpet and paint glowed at him. Why, he asked himself, did I ever marry a decorator?

At the end of the hall an archway opened to a hundred-foot-wide colonnaded garden, fiery red with geraniums and filled by the hissing of a jet fountain and pool at its center. A dark-haired boy of fourteen or so, with dirt-smudged face, dung in the flower beds. Seeing the look on Sam's face, he decided to cultivate elsewhere and departed speedily through a double row of columns at the west end of the building that opened to an exterior park.

A section of the garden-surrounding colonnade had been enclosed by cypress grillwork and converted to a shadowed morning room for one of the larger suites off this courtyard. From there, Sam heard high-pitched giggles.

He walked up to a panel of the grill and slid it aside.

All five feet two inches of Narlo Adamms bounded from a pile of cushions beside Tom's bed and raced for Sam. "Sammy! I thought you'd be late or I'd have been out front with open arms—welcome home!"

"From me too, Sam," came the rasping voice of Thomas Sethy.

Sam ignored Narlo for a second and gazed at the wrinkled old man on the day bed. Even Lifestend failed to preserve him. But into Sam's mind came a vision of the young and wispy-haired writer he had married in 2660. He nearly choked trying to talk around the lump that formed in his throat. Releasing Narlo for a second, Sam knelt and kissed him. "How do you feel, Tom? I stopped by Miami to see Areal on the way home. He sends his love and gave me more Lifestend for you."

An odor of decay, of rot, hung in the room despite its openness and pots of roses.

As Sam rose, Sethy pulled the cover up over his bare chest, hiding its sunken appearance. "How do I feel, Sam? I feel resolved—that's how I feel."

Sam returned an arm about Narlo, still liking the plump feel of him, keeping him close enough to strangle later, and sat down on a love seat facing Tom's bed. Sam knew what was coming next, and dreaded it.

The old man continued, "I desire a last party, Sam. The Lifestend isn't working well anymore, and I feel . . . well, I feel intensely guilty at having access to a drug the rest of our people can't obtain. It's over, Sam. I want a nice final party, but its over now."

Sam let out a sigh, and tightened his grip on the back of Narlo's neck, making the man tremble slightly. But rather than thinking of Tom, he thought of Narlo then. Just how much longer could the standard life-extension drugs maintain the impish Narlo, appearing to be in his late thirties when he was seventy-four? How long before Narlo too had to have Lifestend or fall apart? Even with it, Tom had remained healthy for a mere ten years, then it had left the man only his life, that weak and filled with pain.

Why, Sam wondered, am I this old? Why must I see those I love age, grow feeble, and die, one after the other, and myself look on, an unholy exception. The gay Flying Dutchman!

"All right, Tom. I'll speak to Doc Pulski. We'll have you a grand ball that'll be talked about for a century!"

"Oh, great—!" Narlo began, but Sam crimped the base of his neck.

Rising, but keeping a hand on Narlo, Sam stepped forward and leaned over, planting a light parting kiss on Tom Sethy's dry lips. "I'll return later."

"Thank you for understanding, Sam."

He winked at Tom and pulled Narlo out of the room and

onto the colonnade terrace. Disregarding the little man's screams and protests, Sam picked him up and ran through the open end of the portico. He raced around to the rear of Whitehead Palace, taking the kicking imp out onto the overlook and up to its rail. Flipping him over, Sam held Narlo by one leg out over the drop to the sea, some seventy feet below.

"Aheeee! Oh, no, Sammy! You don't understand, Sammy!"

He snorted. "Then make me understand before my arm gets tired!"

"Please, Sammy. I can't swim!" Narlo squirmed, then realized that this might cause his "lover" to drop him, and stopped still, but for a fast moving tongue.

"Swim? Whale piss! The fall will kill you, Narlo! How much did you spend?"

Gulls circling overhead called down their complaint against such a show. Sam, out of the corner of his eye, glimpsed the gardeners looking on in awe.

"You have no idea, Sammy, how many important people have been arriving in town over the past month! I've never seen anything like it! Two vice presidents of world Corporates. A dozen vice mayors! Ah, Sammy, this place was so tattered. It stank of mold! What if you wanted to have some of these folk up—Aheeee! Oh, please don't kid me like this—I get sooo dizzy!"

"What makes you think I'm kidding? How much?"

The surf produced a drumbeat as it ground at the white marble revetment.

"I only bought a few teeny things that weren't crafted on the island—"

Sam bobbed him up and down violently. "How much!"

In a voice resolved to a long drop, Narlo replied, "Twenty thousand in gold and thirteen thousand Corporate credit units. . . ."

Hauling a trembling and sobbing Narlo up, Sam ran through his mind exactly how much equipment for Sugarloaf and Cudjoe that much money could have bought. Did he even have it in his accounts? Whole cities had been condemned to Exclusion for unpayable debts. Ever since debt had collapsed the great nation-states, fiscal solvency had become the first commandment of world law. And Key West was working itself into a red-inked pit.

Sam buried Narlo's face into his side. He bent over and kissed the top of his head. Tears wet Sam's shirt. "Damn you!"

Behind them, footfalls pounded across the grass. He turned around just as Brio clunked onto the overlook's tile floor.

"How's Gibb?" he asked the panting youth.

After three deep breaths, Brio responded. "Fine, Sam. All settled in. Sam, you gotta come up to your rooms and see Hacker—he's a mess!"

That was all it would take to make Sam's day: a broken cyberbrain, especially one he desperately needed. If anything could detect what this mystical change was, Hacker was it.

Holding Narlo out at arm's length, Sam said: "I'll come to your room tonight, if you still want me to."

"Oh, joy," said with thick tones of sarcasm. But he added, "I've always been a sucker for your body. Mean as you are!"

"Start planning a party for Tom. We can go over the details later—it has to be grand, the works!"

Narlo sneered. "This from a man who nearly killed me for spending a dollar or two!"

"Work out the cost with Agnes."

"I'd rather die!" Narlo sniffed.

Walking off the terrace with Brio, turning his head back toward Narlo, Sam added: "A thousand in gold—max!" Sam shook his head as Narlo returned a broad simper.

He and Brio entered the palace through an arch into the Grand Salon, which Sam noted had reupholstered furniture and new metallic applique worked into the pecky cypress ceiling. Crossing several lesser rooms, they reached and entered an elevator to Sam's second floor apartments.

"He's in your bedroom," Brio said.

They passed through the octagonal living room, stepped down onto a covered terrace to reach the morning room, and entered through French doors into the vast master bedroom. Sam halted in shock just inside the doors. Two gray objects, looking like giant embryos and connected by strands of glassine fiber, lay on the blue sheets of his wide poster bed. As they looked on, the stumpish limbs of these objects lengthened. Sam could see now that the connecting fibers slowly flowed from the object on the left into the one on the right. An odor of hot sand hung in the room.

"He—she's reproducing!" Sam exclaimed, no wonder he hadn't been able to bring Hacker on line. And right when the robot was desperately needed!

Brio closed his mouth, swallowed hard, then spoke: "I didn't know a cyberbrain system could do that."

"Not a word to anyone, Brio." Sam glanced sideways at the darkly handsome face. The youth nodded his understanding.

Hacker and those of his type were the most advanced artificial intelligence system in the world. Their prototype had been designed by Auggy Kittmore. The body was constructed from biolinked silicone controlled by millions of actuator devices to mimic a human body to the finest motion. A cyberbrain composed of billions of neuronet evolvocircuits gave Hacker intelligence surpassing most humans Sam had met, and the machine had learned to invade data banks and security files so fast that it sometimes unnerved him.

But such a high-level system simply didn't adapt to the molecular machine organization—where every molecule of a device was programmably rearrangable—the organization of Areal Silvas's digging robots. Those simpler machines could take in raw building molecules as they dug, then restructure and split into twins. Hacker wasn't a simple digging machine!

Sam had purchased Hacker from Space Construction Corporation, who got him from Auggy's estate, but had never unboxed the robot. Clearly, Sam had bought more than he realized. Auggy Kittmore had designed at least one neuronet system with programming to the molecular level, a feat no one thought possible. Then Kittmore had always been underestimated. In fact, it would not surprise Sam if Auggy Kittmore came back from the grave to eat his enemy's balls!

Sam let out a soft chuckle that caused Brio to stare at him. "Well, I'll have to wait till Hacker Two is born before I can get real news again."

The clank of footfalls on tile caused Sam to wave Brio out of the bedroom; he followed, closing the door. Onto the terrace came a young, gray-eyed Fundy.

"Hail, Samuel. One Charles Pulski says he was summoned. He waits in the entry."

The guard's eyes turned to Brio, and Sam believed he saw a spark of interest. Repression is a terrible control, he thought. "Send the good doctor in!"

The true "doctors" in Key West were clinic cyberbrains. Still, it was nice to have a "Doc" to hold your hand, even a straight-arrow Conch.

He watched the guard return to the foyer and followed Doc Pulski's progress around the wicker furniture and out to them. He carried a thin briefcase tucked under his arm. The man, in his mid-thirties but still with a wiry build, halted just onto the terrace and bowed to Sam.

"I came over as quickly as I could leave the clinic, Mayor. Mister Adamms said you were in desperate need of a tranquilizer."

"Mister Adamms is close to needing a neck splint! Come in and have a seat." Sam turned to Brio and nodded toward the living room. After the youth had left, he said to Pulski: "Tom wants to call it quits."

Pulski brushed his undernourished mustache with a thin

finger. "Well, it is sad, but such is his right. We have a new combination of Lifestend and Easelax called 'Elate' that will restore him to full vigor for a day. But his weakened body can't support it, so he'll die—feeling on top of the world till his last heartbeat."

Sam stared at the tile floor, repressing an urge to vent his wrath against Easelax, but forcing his mind to count the cracks and fall neither into fury nor melancholy. He looked up. "Good. While you're here . . . I'd like an examination."

The man's mouth dropped open; he closed it. "Well . . . I mean . . . I've wanted to do that since the day I began studying medicine. Why now, Mayor? I mean you've said no so many times before."

"I've begun to age." He pointed with the end of his finger to the area of wrinkles under his eye.

Doc Pulski picked up the briefcase from beside his feet, fumbled with the catch, having difficulty opening it with trembling fingers, and tossed back the flap. He took from it a pinky-finger-sized vial of gray liquid and a pint container.

The vial he handed to Sam. "Bioaudit fluid. You drink it, then I collect a urine sample. Your body can keep no secrets from audit fluid, so in an hour—once I feed the sample into our analyzers—we'll know the health of your every organ system and tissue complex."

Sam eyed the polluted-looking contents. He paused a second to listen to the snip-snip of the gardeners below them on the palace platform, to feel the play of warm air over his skin. He shrugged, unstoppered the vial, and drank. The stuff flowed down his throat like cold syrup but with the bitter taste of fresh parsley.

"Many scientists have gone over Perkin Dameral's life-extension formulas . . . nothing. They just don't work, Mayor."

Doc Pulski was referring to the scientist Sam and the Colonel had rescued from World City-State just before Glades turned that place into a giant pool table. The Fundies now made their home in Key West because Dameral had refused to cooperate in developing his drugs unless the Queens' Brigade took the hundred or so mum holies along. After Sam and his men had reached and taken the island from the pirates who then controlled it, Dameral had resumed testing. He used eight subjects, including Sam. Seven died within a week. And Perkin Dameral committed suicide. Sam was still around—a hundred and eighty-eight years later!

"So, you're saying that you have no idea why I'm still alive."

Pulski shook his head. "I wish you had allowed us to examine you before. We would have had a baseline to help measure the changes occurring now."

"Fast or slow—will I age fast, like Tom, or normally?"

"Do you have any Lifestend?"

"One dose," Sam replied, thinking of what Areal Silvas had said—no more. That, on the average, was good for six months.

Doc rubbed at his mustache again. "Keep it close for an emergency. We'll have to audit you once a week . . . perhaps daily. Try to establish a rate of aging—unless the rate's clear from this audit."

Sam rose, took the pint container from Doc, and entered the bedroom. He pissed—bright pink!—in the thing and returned with it. After Doc left, Sam stood alone on the terrace looking out to sea at great, billowing clouds sailing by. But his mind drifted back to a day in 2532, the last day he saw the Colonel. They had argued for a week over keeping the Fundies around; Sam had wanted to give them a boat and wave goodbye. The colonel was furious with him:

"Samuel, you have been like a son to me, far closer than any of the others. I am sad, for you have the body of a fine athlete. The mind of a good commander. And the soul of an earthworm!"

Oh, Sam remembered those words. His ear tips had nearly melted.

"Colonel, the Fundies are as fanatic as any of those in World City-State. They hate who we are!" Sam had yelled.

"Do you think that the bacteria in a termite's gut gives a damn about termites? Hell no! The bacteria cares about a supply of wood pulp. Care or not, hate or not, seperate termite and bacteria and both die. What you're missing, Samuel, is an ability to feel how everything fits together. The whole damn universe is one structure! You still think in terms of little, high-walled boxes."

They had screamed at each other half the night when at last the Colonel's face took on a cool resolve. At the time Sam had wondered if he had decided to kill him, so arctic was his stare. But the Colonel merely said:

"You must learn, Samuel. You will wait here. You will have the burden of managing complex things for a change. Do this till I return."

The Colonel had stormed out of the barracks and vanished. Forever. It had taken Sam all his persuasive powers to convince his fellow soldiers that he hadn't secretly murdered the man.

Sam whispered to the empty terrace. "Well, Colonel. I'm still learning—I hope. And I'm still here, waiting. Do you think my soul's evolved any?"

Brio crouched lower behind a living room couch and held his breath as Doc Pulski walked through on his way to the foyer and its elevator down. So, he thought, Sam Phoe's dying. It won't do me any good to suck up to him! No way I could inherit.

He stuck his head around the corner enough to see onto the terrace. The mayor stood with his back to him, looking seaward. Quietly, Brio got off his knees and tiptoed across the living area and into the elevator foyer. When its doors closed behind him, he let out the breath he had been holding. How much, he wondered, would it be worth to Kenton White to know that his rival was dying?

6

Looking dizzily up into the young soldier's green eyes, Gibb asked, "Is that the password?"

The fellow blinked. Gibb hoped the ritual would end soon; the stone of the plaza made his back ache almost as much as the Fundy's knee hurt his chest. He tried to shift, but nothing worked; his legs had become a web of tingles.

"Don't move!" said the Fundy, as he eased off Gibb and dug through side pockets. He took out a small cylinder and aimed it at Gibb's face, then eyed a device worn on his wrist. "Gibb. Right out of the egg! And drunk. Somebody put you up to this, didn't they?"

Gibb nodded. The soldier waved him to his feet, but when he tired to stand he merely flopped back down, sending a sharp stab up his spine. The Fundy gave him a hand and kept one on his shoulder to help him balance.

The soldier slowly shook his head. "If you'd groped my father or my brother, they'd have killed you. If I report this, Gibb, you'll be tossed off the island! Groping people is customary where you come from?"

"No. It would get and deserve about the same. I'm sorry."

It then dawned on Gibb that he'd been tricked, that Brio held some deadly grudge against him. What had he done to deserve being murdered? He had slept with Lord Sam! Of course, and Brio too was in love with the city-lord. A chill of realization cleared Gibb's head of rum.

"But you won't?"

He tapped Gibb's forehead. "Not if you promise to use this in the future. You're supposed to be in Harsho Jones's charge. Come on. I'll take you there."

Beneath the man's face covering, Gibb thought he detected a smile; regardless, he returned one.

The young man led him to another iron scrollwork pavilion, like the one Brio and he had emerged from after leaving the harbor, and down into the subway system. They took a cart. Its vibrations jiggled his stomach more than he liked, and its high-pitched whine made his head throb, but the dim coolness of the tunnel soothed skin that was too hot. He still felt queasy.

"You're smaller than most of Lord Sam's guards," Gibb said as they slowed to ascend a ramp up to the exit pavilion.

"I'm a girl."

Gibb snapped his head about and studied the Fundy. No wonder "he" wasn't hung, thought Gibb. He could swear that her eyes laughed at him. Noting that his mouth hung open, he closed it. "What's your name?"

"I am called 'Dawn.'"

The instant they came out of the subway, Gibb realized that he was back where he had started: the corner of Duval and Fleming. But she headed in the opposite direction from what he had taken, moving along Fleming, past the place-of-too-much-rum, turning onto a road named "Trumbo." Once past a newer four-story building that occupied one corner, the road became lined with tiny, metal-roofed cottages, surrounded by flower gardens. A number of people passed them, eyeing his companion, saying nothing.

At the end of Trumbo Road they came to twin structures on either side of a gravel lane marked "Via Trumbo." The pair of buildings formed a single hotel—The Alley, said a worn sign—by means of a wooden connecting bridge on the second level; vines with brilliant pink flowers covered it and formed an arch over the via. They passed under and into a lane filled with more tiny cottages and the overpowering scent of orange blossoms. Bright green and yellow birds jumped from tree to tree, squawking as they passed.

Dawn stopped before a fenced compound of three white cottages. "This is the home of Harsho Jones."

"Thanks."

Her green eyes sparkled at him. She reached a hand up, touched his cheek, and ran a finger along it. "God watch over you, Gibb. You certainly need Him."

Gibb waved to the departing Fundy, then entered Harsho Jones's world through a narrow gate. The center cottage jutted forward past the other two. On its porch a brown dog opened one eye, rumbled out a bark as it stretched, and returned to its nap. A rich odor of freshly turned loam drifted to Gibb from twin vegetable gardens at either side of the main cottage.

"Hi!"

A small child with skin the color of chocolate, perhaps three years old, gazed up at Gibb from beneath a water-filled basin raised on a pedestal. He darted over to Gibb. Grabbing his hand, the child stood there looking up at him.

He knelt, asking, "What's your name?"

"Jolley."

Gibb reached out a finger and ran it along the child's petite nose. The little boy giggled.

A creak from dry porch flooring announced a new presence. Glancing up, Gibb saw a thin black woman with smooth and youthful features dressed in an ankle-length white robe, belted in the middle by a blue rope cord. "Hello, I'm Duronea. You must be Gibb. We've been expecting you. Come on in."

Gibb smiled and headed up onto the porch, quickly

Key West, 2720 A.D.

outdistanced by little Jolley. A screen door opened into a living area crowded by wicker chairs and rockers, but Duronea proceeded down a hall that passed the length of the home, lined by exterior windows to one side and by open doors to bedrooms on the other. Past a small kitchen, she went out onto a wide screened porch at the rear of the cottage.

"We were about to eat lunch, Gibb. You hungry?"

Suddenly, he realized what the grinding and growling in his belly was. "Starved!"

Grinning at him, she took an extra plate from a cabinet mounted on the porch wall. Besides little Jolley, three other people sat around a giant table centered in the room. A cradle rested in one corner. The others either smiled or nodded to him.

As Duronea added his plate to the table she introduced everyone. "That's Ron." The man was black, tall and had a distant look to his eyes. "Chub." A pudgy young man with pinkish freckled skin and a wide smile. "And Charlie." She nodded toward a light-shinned woman with towering black hair, who was dressed in a robe so thin Gibb could see pink nipples poking up atop large breasts; she grinned at him shyly. "Oh, over in the crib is Charlie's little girl, Harrah."

Gibb could not help but wonder who went with whom.

"Himself isn't here yet," Duronea added.

"I knew Harsho signed up for the next gay Excluded in," said Chub, "but he never said how you came here."

Duronea set atop the table a massive bowl of beans with large chunks of meat peeking out, then added a basket of light brown rolls, slapping Jolley's hand away from them—Gibb thought he would faint from the aroma! A pitcher and terra cotta cups were already on the table.

"Lord Sam rescued me from a beach in Charlotte's territory."

"*Lord Sam?*" asked Charlie, whose exploratory gaze spoke of nighttime and couples twining between blankets.

Ron shifted in his seat and snorted, "The mayor!"

"Then you were aboard his new ship!" Chub said, eyes wide, elbows on table. "Tell us about it, please."

"Yeah!" little Jolley chimed in.

The attention of so many people made Gibb nervous, yet he began to tell of *Bitch* and the ship's voice, of her great guns that spit fire. But thoughts of the ship brought Brio to mind, dampening his enthusiasm for the tale. he had just begun to speak of the stopover on the Miami River, having omitted his attempt to cut Lord Sam's throat, when a voice from behind him interrupted.

"La, children! The boy's starved to death and you all force him to jaw away his last energy."

Gibb felt a hand on his shoulder.

"Himself," Duronea announced.

Gibb turned about in his chair and looked up into a wide grin. Harsho Jones was remarkably young and thin to have so deep and resonant a voice. Soft-looking, shiny ebony skin surrounded sparkling black eyes. The man wore his raven hair long; it fell to his shoulders, covering the upper part of a white, high-collared tunic, open in the front so that a dark and smooth chest shone through. Chainlike earrings tinkled when he turned his head.

He moved his hand from Gibb's shoulder and rubbed a finger along his face. The man's touch felt cool and soothing. There was something about him that Gibb warmed to immediately. So, apparently, had others, for slowly Gibb began to gather that the household, though of mixed sexes, had but one bull.

"Hummm, may keep you for myself! Boy, you are just plain pretty! See there—you've already turned Charlie's eye, you have."

Gibb glanced over at the woman Harsho teased. She grinned, eyes retreating to her plate. Gibb's own face warmed from a blush.

Harsho moved around the table: He kissed Ron long and deep, pinched Chub's nose, ran a finger down Duronea's neck, and nibbled Charlie's ear.

"Can we eat now, Papa?" asked a petulant Jolley.

Harsho stuffed a roll in the boy's mouth as he passed, returning to take a seat beside Gibb. He tossed a wide-brim white hat, with a long blue feather flopping from it, onto a side table. "Eat up, children!"

Duronea filled a plate with beans, tossed on a roll, and handed it to Gibb. The others, including Jolley, helped themselves. Harsho fished out a hunk of meat and took a roll. With the place knife, he carefully cut open the roll and constructed a sandwich.

"Anybody explain how things work?" asked Jones, after consuming a bite of his creation.

Gibb wondered how much of what Brio had told him came anywhere near the truth. After swallowing a mouthful of the spicy beans, he said, "That I'd be staying with you, working for you . . . for a year."

He reached two fingers over and touched Gibb's arm. "Yes, oh my yes. That's the drift of it. And despite my constant horny state, you ain't a bed warmer. Clear?"

"Yes, lord."

Duronea cut in, giggling, "Woo! Lord indeed—he knows your heart!"

"Quiet, woman! Us men are talkin' business."

Chub, and even the reserved Ron, broke into laughter. Charlie sat with a mile-wide grin on her face. Jolley ignored all of them in favor of dunking pieces of roll into the pot of beans.

"As we were saying, you ain't no bed warmer unless you want to be. And. La! We personally are fully occupied—unless," he allowed a mock glare of regal anger to scan those at the table, "certain of our mates forget their places. Anyway, I run several concession operations for my family—drinks at the stadium and in San Francisco Park. You sell tea and sodas, I pay you two bucks a day. Home and food's free, if you can stand this bunch."

"How much is a drink, sir?" asked Gibb, thinking of the twenty-dollar coin Brio had removed to pay for the rum he had overconsumed.

Harsho scratched his head, looked perplexed. "La! child, but that depends on what and where—"

"Rum."

"Well, over in Samuel Phoe's ultra-expensive Da Vinci Hotel Bar or at the Casa Marina, a buck. Other places, ten to twenty cents, depending on how high class they think they are. You'll be selling soft drinks, though."

Some day, Gibb thought, I'll collect seventeen dollars of change from Brio. And a large section of his hide.

The next morning Duronea stirred Gibb out of a deep sleep an hour before sunrise, fed him and a bright-eyed Harsho a mild fish stew, and had pushed them both out of the cottage door by six-thirty A.M. "House cleaning day," she had said.

As they stood by the front gate awaiting transportation, Harsho said, "Child, what you gotta remember is that Key West is at least half show—for the tourist. Lotta times you'll see some bizarre things goin' on. Likely as not, its show."

He wondered if that applied to Harsho's dress today, for the man wore deep purple satin pants that ballooned widely, golden slippers, and his long hair tucked inside a cylinder-shaped hat with a tassel. His ebony chest was bare, but shone from oil rubbed in by Duronea while they ate breakfast. He carried a fly whisk in one hand. Gibb wore cool white cotton pants and shirt that felt more like Kao's lips than an item of clothing. Chub had insisted he also wear a pink headband—"fly your colors!"—which he did, even though it made his scalp crawl.

"Here they come. La! It's about time!"

Two pair of muscular young men, wearing only trunks and thong-laced sandals came running under the flower dripping archway at the Hotel Alley and toward them down Via Trumbo. Each pair had hold of the ends of a wooden pole, and between these two poles rested a small couch roofed by a betasseled red awning. They halted before the compound gate and set the litter down.

"Now, child, I'll tell you. We coulda walked—good exercise that. We coulda called up one of the little servos to hum us about our business. But a look at prime male flesh gets my juices flowin' better." He pinched the biceps of one dark-haired bearer as they climbed in. "And," he whispered into Gibb's ear, "if they don't get enough business, these beauties either apply to Queens Frat or they reside in the Pits. Sell your ass or live without sunlight, bad choice!"

Even during his short and inebriated stay in Key West, Gibb had noticed the contrast between life aboard *Bitch in Heat*, where the robot ship did every service except wipe your butt, and the city, where people—handsome young men!—provided most services. To feel good about themselves and secure, he guessed, people needed work.

His stomach jumped as the bearers lifted them up and away.

They moved under the deep pink arch of flowers—Harsho whisked at a bee—and onto Trumbo Road. No one stirred. The morning air was still and thick with a sweet scent of flowering plants. The least hint of morning fog weakened distant bright colors into pastels. Gibb's skin tingled with excitement and joy.

Harsho scooted over slightly and placed a warm arm over his shoulder, tweaking his earlobe as he did so. "Your file said you was the only one of your tribe to survive. If you wanta chew it out, I gotta big ear. Just don't let it fester inside ya, okay?"

Gibb hesitated, but he had to talk to someone. "Okay. It's . . . I don't understand. The cities exclude people they don't want inside. There's lots of room between cities for a hard life, scratching at rocks. But the Peakers managed. Why start killing us? What did we have that they wanted?" He felt a lump growing in his throat.

"The first week I was sittin' in the Assembly House, Sam Phoe made a speech—first one in a year. He talked about the SOBs in Glades, said they was grabbin'power around the whole world. They got this grand idea of a world state with them on top o' the heap. With that, they could resettle all the open lands. Once they flush the Excludeds. La! But that wasn't a pretty speech to hear. He was after money for Sugarloaf and Cudjoe—and he got it!"

The litter bearers jiggled them out onto Fleming, also quiet except for one or two merchants unlocking their shops. Harsho waved his fly whisk at them. They gave him the finger.

A group of boys swept the sidewalks before a long string of tiny shops. The oldest appeared to be ten. "Conchs?" asked Gibb.

Harsho's voice took on a sadder tone than Gibb had ever heard the flamboyant man use before. "No. Not every city in the world tosses out gays, most do. Sometimes, wealthier parents have the hormone test run in advance of puberty. And, if their son fails it, 'stead of having the kid tossed at age thirteen by the official test, they send him here. Kind, say!"

Gibb watched the children work, wondered if his own life would have been different if his parents had sent him to Key West before he got the official boot in the ass. "Many of them? I mean, that age?"

"Half the frats have junior branches." Harsho gave him a light shake. "Remember your folks?"

Gibb felt a wave of black fog start across his spirit. He took a deep breath of salt-lined breeze and concentrated on the feel of warm sunshine on his skin. "Sure. My father was a diplomat for Charlotte. When I was eight, we lived in Denver. I liked it there. Something special about the place."

"La, yes! Only city-state in North America that doesn't exclude gays—bless 'em!"

"Why couldn't they have sent me there?"

"Child, Denver keeps its own, not anybody else's. Anyway, you might've found it frustrating. You could be the Kittmore of your generation, but if you like men—you gonna serve tea to the ladies, not practice robotics!"

The bearers trotted out onto Duval Street, under the great, red-flowering trees, and moved toward the overlook where he had nearly gotten his neck twisted. Gibb remembered Dawn and grinned; if ever he developed an interest in girls. . .

"La, just look at these poor Poinciana trees! We make 'em keep a hard-on all year, and won't even let 'em drop seeds on our tiled walkway! I mean how would you like it if you had to keep a hard-on all year and could never cum?"

"Huh?"

Harsho flicked his whisk about, pointing at the great canopy of scarlet flowers. "They're supposed to flower in May, throw down seeds, and make new trees. We fuck with their genes—now they never stop flowering, but never produce a seed—its unnatural!" He winked at Gibb.

"You're like our chief, Onalsey. He had three wives. And me."

"Ah. Yes. Well, I like it that way. My Mammy and Pappy, on the other hand, is pissed. They want a good little gay to warm a seat in the Middle House of the Assembly. They're scared shitless I'll stop loving cute young men and loose that vote." He leaned over and gave Gibb a kiss on the cheek. "Fat chance!"

At the point along Duval where the colonnade before the vast park ran parallel to the street, they met another litter-borne traveler going the opposite direction. A huge ruddy-faced young man sat upright, studying something in his lap. His short red beard glowed in a beam of morning sunlight.

"Stop!" Gibb yelled at their litter bearers.

The other man looked up, saw Gibb, and called a halt to his own progress. His chest was no less wide than Gibb remembered it, his smile no less reassuring. With the rich voice of an ancient cello, he said, "I understand from Cullji Lu that I owe you my freedom, if not my life, Gibb of the Peakers."

"La, who's your hunky friend!"

Before Gibb could introduce him, the man answered, "Alexander of Titan. Most people who aren't trying to arrest or murder me call me 'Pip.'"

"And for all the world to know, I'm Harsho Jones of this rather queer city. 'Pip,' not a term descriptive of your concealed attributes, we hope."

Gibb felt his face heat with a blush.

But Alexander merely smiled, and spoke to Gibb. "You are here. What of your tribe?"

Again a black fog threatened his mind. "They're dead, murdered, sir. All of them."

Alexander of Titan bowed his head momentarily, and when he looked back up Gibb saw in the man's iron-gray eyes a look of fury he had observed in another person only once before. It had been the gaze Onalsey turned on a woman of the tribe who, during that desperate winter of near starvation, had eaten her own baby. The chief's eyes had looked like that before he ordered the woman buried alive.

"I'm sorry, Gibb. At least you made it. I would like more time to speak with you, but I must meet someone at the harbor this morning. Come to the Casa Marina, leave me your schedule, and we'll talk more of this." He turned a grin and wink on Harsho, then ordered his bearers on down Duval toward the harbor.

Harsho reached forward and pulled the ear of the lead bearer. They trotted on.

"La! I could think of a multitude of ways that man could repay me for saving him, all of which would put a dire strain on the island's sheet supply. *You*—tonight—will tell us in great detail how you saved that fabulous muscular hide. Say, Titan—city in Norway?"

"Lord Sam said it's the ninth moon of Saturn."

Harsho thought a moment. The light, quipping tone vanished from his voice. "That's some piece to travel. Somebody in the Assembly commented the other day. . . . Lotta important people sneaking into town under phony names. Not that that's unusual, mind you, child."

They moved into San Francisco Park. The bearers crunched along the plant-lined gravel path amid a sea of flowering shrubs, passing here and there tiny lawns or deep grottoes formed from the root-hung limbs of giant, spreading trees. Thin streamers of fog floated on a mirror lake in the center, and groves of dark-leafed trees partly blocked Gibb's view of distant, terra-cotta-roofed buildings. Tiny birds chirped and darted out of their way. At a juncture of four glaringly white paths stood a frond-roofed hut with a gleaming metal console at its center. In four lounge chairs pulled up under the roof an equal number of boys lay napping.

Harsho cleared his throat loudly.

Startled, two of the boys jumped up and gazed about. When they saw Harsho they grinned sheepishly. The slower two yawned, rubbing at their eyes. The oldest, a thin, sunshine-blond youth, was perhaps sixteen. He wore his hair short but for a high-standing front topknot that seemed to be the style among the young on Key West. Groups of boys with these tufts of hair Gibb had seen in the streets. They reminded him of bevies of quail. This youth's topknot, however, refused to stand up straight, flopping first over one eye and then over the other.

"What do I pay you children for? Sleeping?"

The oldest spoke. Harsho's bite must not be too bad, thought Gibb, for the boy was still grinning. "Ah, Harsh.

There's nobody to sell to this time of morning."

"Hummm. Maybe I should reduce staff."

The oldest slapped his hands together. "Go on, you three. You heard the boss. Go find someone to sell drinks to!" As the others departed—still yawning—down different paths, the young manager came up to Harsho and gave the tall black man a hug. "You mad?"

"La, child! I don't have the time to be angry." Harsho freed himself from the boy, turned, and pointed toward Gibb. "Chip, this is your new supervisor, Gibb."

The boy flashed a grin in his direction while carefully returning his topknot of streaked blond hair to where it belonged. Gibb was in shock from the idea that he should manage something he knew nothing about. "But?"

Harsho held his hands palms out, then reached one back to yank Chip's right ear. "Chip here, you see, might be supervisor now," he turned a raised-eyebrow expression on the boy, "but he's three months and—how many days?"

"Seven," the boy replied, face now beet red.

"And seven days from being legal. His mind—such that it be—floats in a cloud of future lovers and frat choices. So, Gibb, we'll teach you how to sell cheap drinks at high prices, hoping you can keep better control over the business than Chip-the-Horny."

After paying and dismissing the litter, Harsho spent the remainder of the morning showing Gibb how the operation worked. They had one central location, under the hut, where all the mixing equipment resided and to which all one hundred ordering stations located throughout the park were connected. A hatchway to one side of the mixing station led to a storage garage for several dozen servo carts that were used to deliver drinks when the boys were too busy. Gibb caught on quickly, distracted only by the drooling look Chip kept giving him.

"This place's one big bedroom," Chip said, when Harsho

was below counting robots, and with a purring tone to his voice that had only one interpretation. "I mean all sorts of couples come here into the open . . . to make love. It's unnerving."

Gibb asked, "What'd Harsho mean—you becoming legal?"

An expression half-grin and half-agony crossed the boy's face. "Sixteen. An older guy who comes on to anyone who's younger'll get his balls handed to him by a Fundy. There's two crimes a guy can commit on this island that don't ever reach a judge: touch a Fundy or touch a kid. The guys in white'll kill you for either. Everybody, even the tourists, knows it. No problems."

Almost everybody, Gibb thought. The former offense he knew all too well, now. Chip reminded him of Kao; he backed off slightly from the boy. In three months and eight days, he'd think about it. "They sound vicious."

"Not to a kid who's come to a new and frightening place. Wherever he goes on the island, he just has to raise his eyes—there's the white robe. They're distant—we put warmer ice cubes in our drinks." Chip grinned broadly. "After fifteen it's hell waiting! Course, there's always other guys my age, that's okay. God! I like muscles, though, real muscles come attached to older guys."

When Harsho returned, they left Chip and walked on foot around the lake, where aqua-colored sails vied with gold sails in some race as a crowd looked on and cheered loudly. A scent of fried foods drifted to them as they walked, reminding Gibb that the growling in his stomach had a meaning. Harsho halted them near an archway exit between the large structures he had earlier seen at a distance. Wind moaned through them. Here stood a food vendor's hut.

"Oh, James fellow! What gourmet delight have you!"

Harsho handed over a brightly colored ten-cent bill with jumping dolphins on its face in exchange for a scowl from the man behind the counter and pair of wieners wrapped in buns. Afterward, it made Gibb burp, but he was thankful for the fullness in his stomach.

"Like you to come back tonight. Just watch. You can catch a wee nap later this afternoon."

They passed out of the park and into a short via named "Maupin," turning on this toward tile-roofed structures draped by the same purple vines that hung over the entry to Via Trumbo. Nudging Harsho, Gibb pointed at them.

"Bougainvillea. Give them a hard-on too."

At a wide wrought-iron gate with the sign "Casa Marina" above, they entered a people-filled courtyard tiled in yellow and blue geometric designs and surrounded by colonnades of gray-mottled stone. A vast fountain gushed water in the center, cooling the entire area and sending a fine mist floating with the wind. Into their faces. This, Gibb realized, was the place where Lord Alexander stayed.

Harsho led him out through a far end of the colonnade and into an open garden of low hedges covered by tiny sickly sweet-smelling white flowers. "Jasmine," he said without Gibb's asking.

But Gibb's attention riveted to the massive structure in the distance. It was six stories of layered arches, curving gently in either direction along its side, topped by flagpoles waving alternating pink and blue banners.

"Kun Stadium. Concessions I operate in there are more automated. Still, I'll need your help next week. Final match in the cybe wars—no, don't ask; you'll see then. Yours Truly has to serve the VIP boxes. So, you help in the main pit."

They walked up to and through an entry arch that led into a dimly lighted corridor. A side door took them to a set of stairs. Harsho clunked up these to a room filled with shiny metal containers connected by dozens of yellow, green, and blue tubes.

"This here, child, is the gut side of the mixing operation.

Can spit out ten thousand drinks an hour. Not quite fast enough, though."

Gibb didn't understand this comment until the black man took them out of the machine room and behind a sixty-foot-long service counter. The shop was halfway up more rows of seats than Gibb had seen since his vaguely remembered visit to a soccer game in Denver. All the tens of layers of rows bent around in an oval roofed by a giant transparent dome. Its blue light gave the stadium's red seats a purple hue.

"La, child! Forty thousand people, all thirsty! Ah, the money in it!"

"Soccer games?" asked Gibb, not quite certain what type of entertainment occurred below in the giant oval arena.

"Sure. Ballet. Athletic games. Concerts. Holo shows. And the most popular of all—cybe wars!" He put a finger up to Gibb's lips just as the question formed.

Harsho explained the equipment—Gibb's mind was becoming numb from so much detail—pointing out several of the two hundred automated stations spaced among the seats. They discussed the operation here and how it differed from that in the park. Gibb guessed he grasped about half of it.

"Up there," Harsho pointed toward an area where the usual pattern of seating gave way for a box covered by a wide blue canopy, "is where I'll be, helping to serve the illustrious guests of His Honor, Samuel Phoe, Mayor of Key West, forever."

"Forever?"

"Well, to us mortals, it just seems that way."

7

Sam Phoe gazed eastward at a collection of rosy-bottomed clouds, let the salty, chill breeze tingle his face, and tried to clear a foggy mind. He had spent the night with Narlo. They had eaten dinner together and discussed Tom's final party. Sam had insisted earlier that Narlo invite the mysterious Alexander of Titan. And at dinner, Narlo had told him that Alexander had asked to bring a special psych show for entertainment. Narlo had told the man yes, thinking of money saved; but it made Sam the least bit uneasy—what type of psych show? Who travels with such?

In bed, Sam discovered that Narlo had become a sexual madman. Yet, he felt a certain shame in his heart as he made love to him: Even under the most subtle joys Narlo administered, Sam thought of Gibb, of his deep black eyes and smooth body. Nevertheless, Narlo had worn Sam out, then had tossed off into a purring sleep. Sam had no such luck. He must visit Kenton White this morning.

He needed to reach some agreement with Kenton. Agnes Olbo, the city budget director, had outlined the previous afternoon—when not deriding Narlo Adamms—exactly how desperate Key West's and his personal financial situation had become. Between rearming the city's defenses and aiding Excludeds, Sam had amassed for himself and the city a sizable debt.

"And now, Glades has bought up that debt. Do I have to remind you what that means, Sam?" she had said, sitting on the edge of her chair, thin hands folded and supporting her chin, looking like a praying mantis. "No extensions. No mercy. Glades has found a way to level Key West without risking a confrontation with the Latino League. You—and Narlo!—have spent right into their hands. We need a hundred thousand in gold by the end of the month!"

He had mumbled: "I can always sell my CARB stock." (CARB was the Corporate that marketed handmade goods for this area of the world.)

But she had turned so gray that he thought she was having a stroke. "That, Sam, is how you bleed to death!"

She was right of course. He and Areal Silvas were directors of CARB by virtue of the share positions each held. Being a Corporate director afforded both Sam and his city much protection. Corporates had long ago stopped attacking each other, leaving bloody squabbles to the city-states.

Gulls yelled at him as they passed along the retaining wall that kept Whitehead Palace seventy feet above the grinding sea. He reached out a hand to the bedroom balcony railing and gripped its cold metal. Below, three of the grounds staff had come out to continue hand trimming a row of ficus hedge lining the base of the palace's platform. He watched them set up ladders, then remove their shirts to tan while they worked. Are they happy? he wondered. Then he smiled at a bitter thought, remembering Kenton's words last summer: "Who made you everybody's mother?"

"Oh, Kenton! If you had said that to Auggy Kittmore."

That wasn't likely, since Kittmore had died a hundred and ten years before. He had great plans, Sam remembered. Plans to construct a civilization deep in space that would transcend millennia of Earthbound "cultural stagnation." Despite the man's brilliance, he had failed to win over the Corporates, and they poisoned him—in 2610, his dream died with him.

Sam shook himself, left the hemicircular balcony, and

reentered his bedroom, where Hacker and offspring still took shape. They were separate now, taking on final shape by a slow shifting and crawling movement below a "skin" gaining the tone of fine, egg-shell porcelain: twin dolls waiting to be dressed.

To the rear of the bedroom lay a wall cabinet. He approached this with hesitation for the memories it held, stopping before it and standing for several minutes. At last he tossed open its double doors. Inside, the doors were lined with dozens of miniature portraits of the men who had leased his heart over the past two hundred years. He had thought that time would dim their memory; but, as his eyes touched each face, lucid flashes of joy and grief burned at him. Within a day, he must add Tom's face to the gallery, a gallery that had become macabre. Sam reached in, grabbed a message cube from its middle shelf, then quickly closed the shrine.

He strode out of the bedroom into a connecting passageway and entered the comm room. Lights flicked on, for the place had no windows. It was filled with dark brown, padded furniture and moss-green accents. A translucent desk with angled top and with high-backed wooden chair behind it rested in the middle of the floor. Sam sat behind the desk, inserted the cube into a side slot, took a deep breath, and squeaked backward in the chair.

The standing miniature image of a powerfully muscled man with fine buff-colored hair appeared atop the desk. He wore tan slacks and a bright purple jacket. A salmon scarf puffed out from the collar of a lime-green shirt. Smiling to reveal perfect teeth, the man began to speak:

"Sam, love, I know you turned me down when I asked you to leave Key West and join me in the Belt. I can feel your grimace—I won't ask again. No, I'm sending this to let you know that I'll never stop loving you no matter how much distance lies between us.

"You love your city, and I can understand that now. What

I'm building is for the people of Key West, for the tribes of Excludeds, and for any people who still have a soul! In time, you will know what I have done."

Sam watched the figure wipe tears from an eye. The well-aged holo cube sent a loud, hissing pop throughout the den.

Auggy Kittmore continued: "Just remember, there will always be a part of you with me here. A part of you builds with me. Take care of your people. Farewell, love."

In 2599, he had last seen the man alive. The message cube had arrived in December of 2609, a year before his death. A deep sadness descended over Sam as he thought about Auggy. What if he had said yes? If they had worked together on whatever Auggy had wanted to build, could the frightened Corporates have got past Sam's vigil?

Too late now. He had refused from a feeling that Key West needed him—and from fear. Sam knew that he himself had a powerful destiny and a strong will; then he had feared that Auggy Kittmore's aura towered over his own. In Auggy's presence he had always felt diminutive; his ego hadn't liked that feeling. He had built a high wall and puttered in his own small garden when he might have plowed the entire Earth.

"Whale piss! What's done's done."

He shook himself hard. Self-pity wouldn't help him persuade Kenton White to release city funds to him.

Leaving the Palace alone in a small electric cart, he stepped his way down to street level, crossing Conch Plaza before the Spanish-style Assembly Hall and taking a ramp to the lower Lambda Plaza. But in front of the towering, blank-faced Fundy Barracks he picked up an escort; two carts with three men each came whizzing out from between deeply inset steel doors. Morning hymns wafted out with the vehicles.

Sam realized that the Fundies had been one constant in what seemed—until lately—an eternal life. Not once in a hundred and eighty years had he worried about their loyalty. If only the same were true with gays—the main reason for his efforts. The only concern he had about the Fundies now was that they had a new young prophet—their "Prophet of Dawn." A man he should visit, but didn't have the time.

The carts whined along a nearly deserted Truman Avenue, past San Francisco Park with its squawking flights of green and orange wild parrots, past the medical complex. Sight of this brought on a wave of anxiety, which he quickly shoved aside.

On the easterly corner of where Truman met Via Maupin rose a blue and gray wooden Victorian home. Its many wings and octagon towers covered nearly an acre in the center of town. As with most of the old buildings in Key West, it was not on its original site, which was thirty feet underground and back where the Fundy Barracks now stood. People often joked that past mayors built in Key West, but Sam Phoe shuffled.

The carts stopped at the base of a coral-stone retaining wall. Sam motioned for the Fundy guards to remain in the carts and walked up a moss-covered flight of steps. At garden level, a walkway of ancient red bricks led beneath Florida Oaks and between neat beds of just-budding, lavender rain lilies. Another set of steps, these of wood, took him under dripping period gingerbread and onto the porch.

Double oak doors flew open.

"Oh, Sam! It's so good to see you again." The petite woman sprang at him, taking his arm and leading him into a slate-floored foyer that echoed every word. Lillian White's gray-streaked blond hair came to the level of his chin. She turned a beaming face up to him. "Kenton will be down in a moment. I told him to set an alarm, not to oversleep. He never listens."

He trotted out his biggest grin for Kenton's mother. "How have you been, Lill?"

She let go of his arm once they had gained the green and gold brocaded parlor and pointed at a massive padded chair. It was the one she had ordered installed in the room when she knew Sam and her son had formed a relationship. "Big men need big chairs," she had said, with a dimpled grin.

"Tea?" she asked as she sat upon a narrow bench drawn up close to his chair.

He nodded. Lillian clapped her hands, and a thin black man in crisp white livery appeared at the archway that connected to the dining room. A massive crystal chandelier glittered in the background above a polished walnut table for twenty. The man brought in a silver tray groaning under the weight of teapots, creamers, and dishes of strawberry tarts—Sam's favorite. After placing the morning tea on a low table between them, the servant departed.

"I'm all right, Sam," she said while pouring him a cup, adding the single lump of sugar he had always requested. "But I would be much better if you and Kenton were together again. He's stubborn, Sam!"

"So am I, Lill."

"Well," her face wrinkled with a frown, "age has its privileges. . . . At a mere thirty-three he doesn't deserve many."

She took a delicate sip of her tea. Sam did likewise, wolfing a tart with as much grace as his empty stomach would allow. He could detect the flavor of sweet orange juice she always added to the recipe to contrast with the strawberries.

"Every Sunday, Sam, I pray that the two of you will get back together. Both of you love our city. You should love each other!"

Sam was trying desperately to think of placating words, when a feigned cough interrupted.

"Do I detect a conspiracy in the making?"

A bright-eyed and smiling Kenton White stood at the foyer entry wearing baggy blue pants and an unbuttoned coral-colored shirt that revealed most of the man's smooth and tawny chest. With a level of grace Sam couldn't achieve with a year's practice, Kenton walked over to them, bent and kissed his cheek.

"There! You see. You two can make up, if you want to."

"Yes, Mother. *Anything* is possible." Kenton winked at her.

But Kenton's tone caused Lillian White to purse her lips. She said nothing more, rather merely escorted them through the foyer to the doors into the study. Once they went inside she looked at the men, began to say something but thought better of it and closed the double red-lacquer doors.

Alone among a collection of oriental antiques, Kenton spoke first: "How was your trip to Albany?"

Sam took a seat at one end of a low, overstuffed couch; he bent and patted the far end. The younger man joined him. "Going up there always leaves a bitter taste in my mouth. But I think we'll have an emigration treaty with Denver by the end of the year."

"Great!"

The two men never argued over ways to bring new gays to Key West. It was a gay city, and had been for over seven hundred years. And since gays don't breed more gays, and even though the city became overcrowded at times, they agreed on opening multiple pathways for new Lambda citizens.

Rubbing an index finger along the couch back, not looking at Sam, Kenton asked, "Any new hope about getting us city-state status?"

"Dead issue. I suspect that Glades calls the shots now for nearly every city in North America. Even the Latino League has backed off its support for us." He reached over and gently placed his hand atop Kenton's wrist. The smooth warmth of his skin sent a shiver up Sam's spine. "Why have you cut off money for Sugarloaf and Cudjoe?"

Kenton White sat up straighter, removing his hand from under Sam's grip. His eyes sparkled. "I, Sam, am not the mayor. The Assembly cut off funds! The people cut them off! Do you think any of us likes what Glades is doing to the Excludeds? No!"

"Then why not help?"

Kenton stared directly into his eyes as he spoke. "Sam, it goes beyond money, even though that's getting too tight for comfort. Glades is behind an almost worldwide push against the Excludeds' tribes—"

"How do you know that?"

Kenton folded his arms across his chest and glared. "You won't tell us anything about world affairs, so we opened our own channels. Sam, Glades is too powerful to cross or tease, as you love to do! You continue to house Excludeds against Glades' wishes, and they will shit on Key West, if we're lucky and they don't blast us below sea level! Back off of this and they'll leave us alone, collecting the wealth of taxes we pay them—"

"Like hell they will!" Sam rose and paced before his ex-lover. The wooden floor squeaked as he walked. "You've never met Jacksen Lear Sudger the Third."

Kenton threw his head back and snorted a short laugh. "I wonder whose fault that is? Happens that I spoke with the man yesterday, over the holo. When you bypassed the courts and had your Fundies toss out those Glades police agents, I felt obliged to apologize."

Sam turned slowly and stared at the man in disbelief. Blood drained from his head, yet the tips of his ears felt as if they might melt and flow off his head. He spoke in a measured voice: "A minor incident that Sudger might never have been informed of, you have hot-lined in fluorescent orange!"

"What interest do we have in deep space rebellions? Why would we further anger Glades over this? I discovered at whose request you intervened. Sam, really!" He tilted his head to one side and smirked. "Getting Key West stepped on just to make your new piece of ass happy!"

Sam's facial muscles clenched so hard that his head began

to throb. He concentrated all his thoughts on the warm and sweetly expectant face of Lillian White. Only that image kept him from killing her son.

Quieter than he thought possible under the circumstances, Sam turned his back on his ex-lover and left the ancient home.

Black thoughts accompanied him all the way to the palace and into the den of his private apartment. He was furious at Kenton's crack about Gibb; the boy was guilty of nothing but surviving and remembering those who had helped him. Sitting behind the tilted glassine desk, he called Uriel Fordac. The Fundy's slightly transparent, white-robed image appeared before him in the room.

"Hail, Samuel!"

"Captain, I want Kenton White. . . ." He reached the precipice and nearly went over, yet some last ounce of integrity stopped him. In another second he would have ordered his ex-lover arrested. That would prove the man right and make a mockery of what Sam Phoe believed himself to be. "I will not become a tyrant!"

"Pardon, Samuel?"

"Nothing. Thank you, Uriel."

He clicked off the holo and took several deep breaths. These failed to remove a ringing in his ears. He rose and stretched, bringing a sudden and sharp pain to his groin. "Ouch!" Had he pulled a muscle in storming from Kenton's house, leaping down the stairs? A small star of red blinked on one corner of the desk.

"Text."

A message from Doc Pulski appeared on the angled surface:

> MISTER MAYOR, I HAVE RUN SEVERAL TESTS OF THE GENETIC COMPONENTS FROM YOUR CELL AUDIT. THOUGH A FEW MORE ARE NEEDED, I FEAR THE NEWS ISN'T GOOD SO FAR. THE AGING PROCESS IN

> your body is unstable. Please keep the vial of Lifestend near you until I complete the tests.

Sam would never use Lifestend! It was habit forming and eventually turned on its users, as it had turned on poor Tom. Sam Phoe began to doubt his own sanity: part of him suddenly suggested that he reconcile with Kenton and train the young man to take his place. Moments before, he would have strangled him. These wild gyrations of emotion made him dizzy.

An odor of hot sand wafted into the room.

"Pardon, Mayor."

Sam looked up at the two porcelain figures who stared at him with the eyes of dolls. That they saw nothing through these cosmetic eyes—elaborate sensor networks provided the robots with an energy wavelength map of all about them—never seemed to matter; the impression of human attention was complete.

"Are you finished splitting in two?" Luckily, machines merely noted a sharp tone of voice, but didn't take umbrage. Or did they? But then *Bitch* didn't count.

"Quite, sir. We have processed the backlog of requests filed with *Bitch in Heat* earlier. The deep space rebellion tops the stack. Do you prefer hard copy, or shall we discuss the data?"

Sam leaned back in his chair and eyed the twin machines; each was shorter and thinner than Hacker used to be. "I didn't think neuro-net systems could reproduce."

"It was an unexpected event for Hacker too, sir," the machine on Sam's right said.

He pointed at this one. "Can you form three green chevron stripes on your chest?"

The right-hand machine's evenly rounded front altered color to a heraldic vert, which then whittled away to sergeant strips at dead center.

"Keep that so I can tell you apart: Private and Sergeant. What's the current status of the rebellion?"

Private began in a high voice, but adjusted it lower as if trying to approximate Sam's tone. "The rebellion is now ten years old. However, all files we tested refer to actions in deep space as a *war*. Only public relations information uses the term *rebellion*. Files released to the various city-state managements note a six-month-old breakdown in communication beyond the orbit of Mars as due to unusual sunspot activity. On the other hand, Solsys files mark these areas as 'lost to the enemy.'"

"Whale piss! You mean the Corporates are fighting a major war in deep space and even the city-states are unaware of it?" Sam rubbed at the scar on his chin and tried to quell a growing sense of panic. Any change in the balance of power was a danger to the fragile status of Key West. "Who is the enemy?"

Sergeant spoke, "Some files refer to Titans, others to a Confederation. It seems clear that Solsys doesn't know the face of those who oppose it."

"No mention of a 'Starcastle'?" Sam asked, remembering the name Gibb had heard.

"No, Mayor. You had requested information on attacks against tribes of Excludeds. They are decreasing . . ."

Good news, thought Sam.

". . . but apparently not because of any reduction of activity by the world's city-states. A chart of tribal movements in North America over the last ten months is illustrative of worldwide patterns."

A picture of the continental territory appeared on Sam's desk top. The twelve city-states of the old USA slashed across the map from northwestern-located Spokane to Glades in the southeast. The cities were red dots on a green map with the population of Excludeds represented by a bluish hashing spaced well away from the cities.

"Perfect circles," Sam mumbled to himself. "But then if someone had been feeding the tribes, they wouldn't need to raid croplands close to the cities. But—perfect circles?"

Private responded, "With a mode of two hundred miles from the central structures of any city-state or major metropolitan installations. Worldwide, these circles vary by only five miles of diameter."

A shiver passed though Sam's body. *Coordination*, he thought.

He raised a hand to silence the robots, and entered a code at the desk-top key pad for World-News. The holo flashed on; a smiling beauty of a young man dressed in loose shirt and baggy pants appeared against the far wall. The news agency long ago had gotten Sam's number, always generating an image to his taste. The news was accurate so long as it was mostly social, or the Corporates wanted it spread; otherwise, it was pure propaganda. Yet, when his hacking robots tuned in they could trace backward into World-News's data base and either find the truth or approximate it.

"Hello, Sam," said the handsome, computer-generated image. "It's been a while since you've called. Do you wish tourist info or general news?"

"Starcastle."

"Pardon."

"I want any data you have on the term 'Starcastle.'"

The image rubbed its chin. His request was drawing a detailed search, and he hoped the file wasn't so blocked that his hackers couldn't gain entry.

With a wide smile on its face, the computer image at last spoke: "A myth, Sam. It's a myth of the Belt, somewhat like El Dorado, except that it is a place where those men lost in space go—a heaven, if you will."

A copper taste in his mouth signaled Sam that the hackers had all they needed. He flipped off the news channel. "Well?"

Private spoke: "The report is correct, though incomplete. On seventeen September twenty-six twenty the mining ship *Bedford* sustained severe damage in a meteor storm while operating in an isolated area of the Belt. They were without engine power and were losing atmosphere; no ship was close enough to rescue them in time. Or so they believed.

"But a ship did come to their aid. The miners later reported that the craft was so immense that, at first, they thought they had made contact with an alien starship. Those aboard the helper ship reinforced this idea by never showing themselves or communicating. Robot servos repaired the *Bedford*, and the unidentified giant craft departed.

"All the *Bedford*'s recording devices failed to provide any information; they had been erased. One member of the crew who went outside on the hull of *Bedford* saw the other ship's markings: a castle piece, as used in chess, atop a five-pointed star. Such human symbols removed any thought of alien manufacture."

Starcastle," Sam mumbled to himself. "How large did the miners claim this other ship was?"

"They were laughed at, but apparently stuck to their estimation of three miles long—"

"Three miles!" His mind spun. Even allowing for exaggeration, any space ship approaching that size would have to derive from a considerable industrial base, larger in fact than anything that was in space—or known to be in space.

"There have been sixteen similiar incidents in the past ninety years, always the same, no contact," Sergeant added. "The Belt miners broadcast to Starcastle constantly."

"Any answer?"

"No. That is, nothing beyond assistance when it's most desperately needed. Still, Solsys dismisses the matter as a myth created by lonely miners."

Sam felt exhausted. He had spent too much time over the last ten years trying to brown-nose city-state status for Key West and dodge the evil intent of Glades, and not enough paying attention to worldwide issues. At least there was a source of information in Key West: Alexander of Titan.

Another thought occurred to him. "I want you two to dig

Key West, 2720 A.D.   *105*

out every file on Augustus Alvin Kittmore, especially information on his activities during the last ten years of his life. Violate any data banks you must—including those at Glades, regardless of the risk—but prove or disprove a connection between Kittmore and Starcastle."

Later that day, Sam sat on the palace overlook reviewing final plans for Thomas's party with Narlo and trying not to let the pain in his stomach show on his face. Sergeant walked onto the terrace with an update—Narlo giggled at the chevron, saying he'd always liked men in uniform.

"Proposition solved?" Sam asked.

"Not Yet, Mayor. But we thought you should know: Yesterday at eight-thirty A.M. all communication with the Mars colonies halted."

The statement caught Narlo's attention. "Sam, what does that mean?"

"Sunspots, Narlo. Just sunspots." But all of Sam's being wanted to scream: *It means change!*

8

Gibb moved along Duval Street against a tide of people heading in the opposite direction toward Sea Plaza and the docks. They flowed like a spring flood to attend the ritual observation of sunset, or so Harsho had told him. But he had half an hour to reach the park. Yet, his attention constantly locked on the items for sale in the shop windows—carved seashells; perfumes whose scents of love-on-a-tropical-night wafted to him; holographic art: a surfer forever catching the right wave; clothing so colorful and desirable as to threaten the wealth jingling in his pocket. And the odor of grilled meat.

Duronea had offered some leftover fish stew at the house, but a stomach filled with dandelion fluff forced him to decline. Other than survival, Gibb had never held a job before. It made him nervous.

Halfway to his goal, the fragrance of the same bun-wrapped wiener he had eaten at lunchtime stirred his appetite. Stopping before a food cart, Gibb watched an older man with a crooked smile piece together the sandwich. He ordered every topping in sight. Gibb handed over a silver coin.

The fellow scowled at him, digging first into one cash box, then a second located under the cart. Handing him his change, he said acidly, "What are you? One of the merchant princes of the world!"

Key West, 2720 A.D.

Gibb wasn't quite sure what he had done to disturb the man; he shrugged it off and walked on along the street. Different areas of the vast, tree-canopied walkway vibrated with their own music, which he walked into and out of within a dozen paces: one minute a choppy and surging beat, the next a grandly explosive sound from hundreds of instruments. But the many musical moods never mixed. Crowd noises stood between these cones of rhythmic expression.

He left the sidewalk and strolled out under a great pink-flowered poinciana at a spot where a dozen small tables clustered around a three-tiered fountain. The gentle plucking of a harp replaced the roar of people as if he had stepped inside an enchanted cave. A snaking dance of nearly naked men and women pounding at small drums wound silently between the spreading trees near where Gibb sat. The effect was spooky, like watching ghosts twirl by.

Idly, he removed the change the hot dog seller had handed him and began sorting through it: ten brightly colored paper bills printed with seashells or pink sunsets or sailing craft fighting high waves, to a total value of $4.95; one silver five-dollar coin sporting the up-side-down "y" on it; and a ten-dollar coin with a man's face. Samuel Phoe's face.

A wave of melancholy washed over Gibb. He tried to tell himself that most of Key West was in love with Sam Phoe in one way or another, but such logic didn't ease the ache. He felt a clawing at his heart. To be with the man would be enough, even if they never made love again. Still, Gibb trembled at the thought of Lord Sam's gentle touch, a caring touch he had never known before.

Gibb wolfed down the last bite of hot dog while he could still swallow and shook himself free of self-pitying thoughts. He had a job.

When he reached the park, its lighting had just come on, providing starlike speckles in a bluish gloaming. Young tourist couples crunched by him on the pink and white pea-gravel paths or lay on rented blankets watching the rosy western sky. Some, more secluded by plantings of ficus hedge or sawgrass, made love. From these scenes, Gibb looked quickly away; they made his groin pulse. Something he didn't need before spending a shift with Chip the Illegal.

Those at the stand worked feverishly. Gibb hadn't observed that many customers. He inquired of a grinning Chip, whose left hand fought a losing battle with his rebellious topknot.

"Lots of people come at sunset to watch the sky, sip hot tea, and fuck. Like mating hour!" Gibb felt heat from a blush on his face, which made Chip grin all the wider, stop work, and slip closer to him. The boy pinched his biceps and said: "Wow! Lots of muscle for a thin guy. How old are you?"

"Eighteen." Gibb changed the subject, knowing that adventure would distract any fifteen year old: "Let's work the machines, and I'll tell you about my trip here on the Mayor's ship."

Luckily the strategy worked.

At midnight, he said goodbye to Chip and the other six boys manning the operation and walked out of the park via its Duval Street exit. All the city's lights had dimmed by half; he guessed this brought to higher effect the holographic light show of multicolored, flowing shapes that twisted and turned above in the night sky. Working with the incurably optimistic younger boys had lifted his spirits and a caressing salt breeze seemed to say that in this magic city all endings were happy, every wild dream fulfilled.

Rather than turn toward the harbor and distant Trumbo Road, Gibb went toward the overlook. He crossed into the small plaza, walked around the column with its bronze statue of a man in military uniform, and stopped to lean against the stone balustrade. The tide-pushed sea thrashed thirty feet below him, pounding at the stone wall. He bent over and, in the flickering red and orange of the light show, noticed that the wall was far less even than he had believed. In fact, virtual stepping stones jutted outward here and there along it. If ever he wanted secretly to visit Lord Sam's high palace....

"Don't jump. It isn't that bad."

Startled, Gibb jerked about and stared into soft green eyes, all of the girl's face that showed. Her white uniform reflected a hellish red glow from the twisting strands of light in the sky. "Greetings, Dawn."

"Greetings, Gibb-once-of-Charlotte. How do you find the household of Harsho Jones?" As she spoke, she unwound the cloth from about a thin and beautiful face with smile-warmed lips.

"Strange. Fun."

She expelled a musical laugh. "Harsho is a strange man. With three doctorates, he is perhaps the best educated young man on the island. Yet he plays the clown! He is fun to watch and listen to, but I think his heart is the least strange I know."

Gibb changed the subject.

"You never seem as intense as the other Fundies. I mean in guarding things and watching." He hoped his words didn't offend her; it was through her understanding that he lived at all.

She turned her gaze seaward. "Intense. Oh, but I am, in my own way. My father doesn't quite know what to do with me. As God wills it, I see things the elders don't. I feel things they don't. So, he cannot merely confine me with the other women, forever looking at our private landscape. He dresses me like a boy, then pretends I am one."

"What do you see?"

"The hand of God. His fist. It's coming, and much that you see here," she waved a hand across the inky horizon, "will not survive."

The tone of Dawn's voice put a lump in his throat and sent a shiver down his spine. In the high forests of the Peakers, Gibb had heard of those who knew the future, knew the will of God. They were much feared and shunned.

"You are beautiful," he said, not sure why, perhaps again to change the subject.

The young woman turned back to face him. Her visage altered from distant gloom to girlish mirth. "That's nice to hear, even from a sodomite." Gibb didn't like the term, yet her tone was playful and not filled with scorn. "Most of the young men of my people think me too odd for what beauty I have. And I never enter their minds—at least not in that way."

"I meant what I said. Your face is perfect."

She grinned at him. "Disinterest is always a good judge."

Gibb thought it unwise to tell her just how interested he could be.

"Have you visited the Church of the Secret Lover?"

Gibb hadn't heard of it, much less visited it. He shook his head, and she motioned for him to follow her. Could this be an invitation to something, he wondered? Secret lover? If he ever made love to this girl, it had better be a secret!

Back along Duval Street in the small half-block before crossing Casa Marina Way, stood a blank-faced building. Only a carved marble archway gave hint that more than a warehouse waited within. But through this was a four-sided and columned arcade the walls of which contained statue-filled niches every six feet. A purple glow from the light show flowed in through a wide opening above a courtyard.

Dawn waved her hand in a circular motion, indicating the recessed statues. "Your people's heroes." She moved across the courtyard and between beds of shadowed flowers without stopping.

At the far side a set of wooden double doors led inside a large room. Lighted by a hundred flicker-tipped candles that left the place smelling of wax and burnt wick, it was disappointingly plain. Unadorned windows made openings in whitewashed walls of unfinished concrete block. Benches formed two rows on either side of a wide aisle that rose slightly to a pulpit some fifty feet away. A cross of light-colored wood

hung on the wall behind it. The ceiling was low and confining. Dawn sang softly:
> YOUR HAND IS HIDDEN BEHIND THE STORM'S FURY
> YOUR ANGER VIVID FOR ALL TO SEE
> YET ONLY YOUR LOVE IS CLEAR TO ME. . . .

From the story of Preacher John that Lord Sam had told him, Gibb realized where he was. "This is the church! I mean where the people of Key West came to pray during the great storm."

Dawn nodded. Her face appeared serene and remote in the yellow light. "He's still here, Gibb. His presence tingles every nerve in my skin the minute I walk into this church." She absently reached a hand up and ran it along her cheek. "I . . . tried to tell the elders that He was here. They said it wasn't true. They said that God resides within our seamless walls, protected from the sight of the vileness of Key West without."

Gibb watched tears begin to pour down her cheeks. She did not wipe them away, and so when she turned to face him, they glistened and sparkled in the candlelight. He said: "Maybe God has just returned here."

Dawn shook her head. "We were brought to Key West to learn a lessen. We have failed."

Gibb stayed with Dawn in the Church of the Secret Lover for half an hour more, then left her to pray, as she did every night. Some of her sadness had rubbed off onto him, and so when he reached Duval, he walked back inside the park to avoid the throngs of people still shopping and partying. He strolled around the lake on the side opposite Harsho's concession stand and the ardent Chip, aiming for the archway out onto Via Maupin. A lone figure on a bench caught his eye.

The man sat with his head buried in his hands; low sobbing from him rose above the background chittering of crickets. Gibb watched a minute, then approached half a step at a time, drawn by recognition of the silhouette. Ghosts haunted his mind. He stood over the man, trembling, chest tight from some cold-handed grip, and with lungs aching from breaths not taken.

At last noticing he had a visitor, the man said, "Please, leave me alone. I am not here for pleasure."

But when Gibb didn't move, he looked up with wet, unrecognizing eyes. "What do you want?"

"Father?"

The man stood and gaped at him, rubbing a trembling hand across curly but thinning hair. "Gibson? How. . . ?"

"I survived, Father. No thanks to you." Gibb felt a blaze of hate flare from five years of struggle and deprivation. But in two heartbeats a numbing set it.

Russell Makkle stood in silence, staring at his son. He made no reply to Gibb's accusation. Yet Gibb saw the faint lines of a smile replace the agony that had been on the man's face. Whatever his troubles, the sight of his son hadn't added to them. "You are a man, but in your face I can still see the little boy I knew. That you are well will be welcome news to your mother, Gibson."

Faint giggles and the scent of blooming plants floated to them on a puff of salty air.

"Why are you here, Father? You like boys?"

He wiped at his eyes and grinned at Gibb. "The way my mission here is going, I wish I had been excluded at thirteen! In fact, after this trip I may well be."

Gibb nearly choked on the words that he had to ask: "Father, why didn't you send me here? You must have known about this place—it's only by God's will that I'm alive!"

Russell Makkle carefully studied the gravel path at his feet before replying. "To have a son fail the hormone test was a black mark on my record. To have sent you to Key West would have sounded a death knell for my career—an admission of weakness! I was ambitious. Can you understand?"

"Did it gain you anything?"

The man looked at Gibb again and brushed at missing hair. "I am Under Secretary of State for Charlotte now. At least I am until I return from this mission!"

"You came to see Mayor Phoe?" asked Gibb.

He let out a snorting laugh. "Good Lord, no! We would never deal with him. I can't say much. There is a foreign ambassador in Key West. My goal—secret even from the President of Charlotte—is to negotiate certain understandings with him. I've failed so far, Gibb. He is one hell of a hard man." His voice lowered and his gaze appeared to loose focus. "I've never seen such fury in a man's eyes.

"Son, I must go. Where do you stay?" Russell held out his hand to Gibb, not quite daring to look the boy in the eye.

Gibb hesitated a second, torn between hate for all the hardships and violence he had been forced to endure from age thirteen on and memories of his earlier childhood when the man before him had been warm and loving. He took the proffered hand, then closed and hugged him. "Tell mother I love her."

After Gibb gave his father Harsho's address, they parted company. All of the mental walls he had built between what he was now and what he had been as a boy came crashing down with such force that his hands trembled. Gibb's emotions were shards.

That night his sleep was troubled by dreams of childhood and by nightmares of the Peakers and blood and by Kao's lonely death on a deserted beach. With morning his worries expanded.

Duronea tapped at his door around nine and handed in an envelope contained a letter from his father, written in a Charlotte cipher he had forced Gibb to memorize when he was eight. It read:

Dear Gibson,
Today I shall open an account in your
real name at the SwissCent Bank branch

located in the Hotel Da Vinci. As soon as I return to Charlotte, I will make arrangements with officials in Denver who owe me favors so that city will accept you.

I did not help you when you were younger. There is no excuse this time, if there was years ago. You must not remain in Key West, for it is only a matter of weeks at most before Glades destroys it.

Love,

Your Father

Gibb folded the thick paper and laid it on his bed. Whatever his father might think, Gibb's loyalties ran far deeper. Only one thought crossed his mind: *Lord Sam must see this letter!*

9

Brio paced distractedly in the cone-ceiling living room of Sam Phoe's private apartment. He made loops in and about the wicker chairs and love seats, looking at an ancient cuckoo clock with each pass. He would walk to the Hotel Walt Whitman at eleven—just an hour away—but he didn't want to show up early.

Flopping in a chair beside the holo table, Brio took several deep breaths to calm his shaky nerves. The idea of talking to a Glades agent left him uneasy despite the money it promised.

He dug in the pocket of the shorts he wore and took out the "ship"—a two hundred dollar gold coin with a sailing craft on its obverse. Kenton White had paid him well enough for knowledge of Sam Phoe's illness. Still, he hadn't smiled at Brio once. White had dealt with him as if he had been taking out garbage. That had pissed off Brio to the point of making contact with people who were known on the island and usually avoided.

Ting.

"Yes." Brio stood as he answered the holo.

A twirl of light formed above the table, then took the shape of a white-uniformed Fundy. The man's eyes appeared accusing. "I seek Samuel."

"He's still sleeping." That was true. Cramps had kept the mayor awake most of the night.

The guard hesitated a second before continuing. "One Gibb, a Lambda without fraternity, seeks an audience with the mayor—"

After a second of shock that the kid had survived, Brio broke in: "Sam doesn't wanta see that one!"

"You are sure? This Gibb says that his business is urgent."

Thinking of what Gibb might say to Sam about him, Brio snapped out authoritatively: "It's a ruse! Sam will never wanta see him."

The Fundy shrugged and vanished.

That was close, thought Brio.

It was early, but he didn't want to be waiting around if the guard should call back. He took the elevator down and left the palace through the western atrium courtyard. A chilling light mist competed with a waning sun for control of the day, making the park landscape indistinct and uncertain. Brio ran to the arcade built inside the northern seawall. He shook himself off before echoing along this to a steel postern and stairs beyond. The gate hummed aside for him, and he took the steps down two at a time until he reached the far corner of Lambda Plaza. Avoiding Duval Street, Brio cut through the pines of Queens' Park, immediately off the plaza. Its carpet of wet needles squished under foot and attacked his nose with a resinous odor.

His shirt and pants had become soaked. A chill began to rattle his teeth as he entered the western nib of Fleming bordering the Walt Whitman.

The hotel's flat wall was composed of filled arches on the first two floors that gave way to sets of French doors and balconies on the four levels above. Yellow awnings flapped in the wind, dumping water down onto Brio's head. *Shit on again!* he thought. He would not look presentable this morning; there was nothing he could do about it.

Inside, the fiercely shining marble lobby echoed his squishing steps. The doorman gave him a disparaging look. Brio had a room number—603—and no name; so, the elevator detained him until it inquired of the room's occupant if the boy were really expected. He was. Before the suite's carved oak doors, Brio's resolve crumbled in an avalanche of trembling regret. He turned away.

A staccato voice stabbed his back. "Where you goin', kid?"

Brio halted, his stomach falling away. He turned about and saw a pot-bellied man with a hundred times more hair on his body than he had on his head. A bright pink towel wrapped his middle. The youth approached him. "I'm—"

"Yeah, sure. I know who you are: Brio Dirrenni, the mayor's aide and general piece of ass—"

"I'm not—"

"Yeah, yeah. You're early. How'd ya get so fuckin' wet? Come on in. You can call me 'Billy.'" After the man let Brio through and slammed the door shut, he crossed the suite's foyer and entered a bedroom suitable for Whitehead Palace. The unshaven Billy contrasted poorly with elegant gold brocades, mellow oaks, and polished crystal. They moved into the bath. "Sit on the john lid there while I shave."

Brio sat, feeling uncomfortable, and watched Billy apply a coating of razor cream over a pocked face.

Allowing the cream to set, he leaned against the sink and leered at Brio. "Strip out of those soppy clothes, kid."

He complied. That the agent might want more from him than information had never occurred to Brio. The thought produced a chill unrelated to the damp things he had taken off.

"Not bad looking, for a fag. Girls never interest you?" He looked back to the mirror and began washing off cream and black specks of beard.

"No. I—"

"Yeah, yeah. I know—you're a girl yourself. Ha! Without the right equipment, huh?" The man dried his face. He walked over to Brio and pinched a nipple. It hurt.

Speaking quickly, praying he could steer matters back to

business, Brio said, "I have information about Mayor Phoe's health that'll—"

Billy raised a hand to stop his flood of words and motioned him back into the bedroom. He placed a finger against the glass surface of a painting hanging near the giant bed. A cube of wall slid forward. It was a safe drawer. He reached inside and pulled out an elongated pouch, heavy-looking by the way it strained his wrist. Unzipping it, he grabbed something into his hand.

"Now, kid. What we want from you is special info. Very simple info. We want the full set of security codes for Kun Stadium."

A whirlwind of fear and wild speculations twirled through Brio's head. "I. . . ."

Billy thumped a stack of gold coins onto an oval breakfast table, knocking over a petite flower vase. "Three thousand dollars gold, now. Three thousand more when our job in the stadium is done. What say, kid?"

Brio stared at the dull yellow stack: more money than he had ever seen in his life. A thrill surged through him from the thought of what six thousand gold dollars could buy. A house. A business. His return to Rome!

Brio nodded.

"Good kid! All you need do is get hold of the codes and transmit 'em here to my room." He shoved the stack toward Brio. When the youth grabbed the coins, Billy grabbed his ass. "I gotta try once, kid. While this pansy patch is still around."

Brio winced from a violating finger. The man's body stank of stale oil. "No, I—"

"Yeah, yeah. You'll love it, honey!" The man's grip was unbreakably hard.

At one point during an hour of jack-hammering, Billy whispered in Brio's ear: "Cross us, honey, and I'll fill your sweet asshole with lye!"

10

De Obeyua's *Symphony for a Hundred Bottles* hummed and vibrated throughout the mosaic-floored reception hall (Sam had ordered Narlo's expensive new carpet returned to the store). Sam found the music depressing; written in 2134, its sad flow of notes bespoke flooded cities and death and the confusion of crumpling governments. It was Tom's choice.

The liveried household staff rushed about placing or replacing terra cotta pots of yellow mums, orange bird of paradise, or great crystal bowls of fragrant white magnolias. All under Narlo's franticly waved directives. An aroma of freshly baked bread drifted in from the north hall, where the staff had decided to set up a buffet for Tom's eighty or so guests. The state dining room could seat only half that number.

Sam sat in one of the new *fauteuils* wondering how Narlo managed to accomplish anything amidst so much confusion. All day he had felt better, the pains had subsided, and this made him more at ease for the party. He glanced about for Brio, who had been missing all day. Perhaps the youth couldn't stand the idea of a final party for someone. Many couldn't. Sam's gaze went to the twenty-foot-high double pocket doors to the Music Room as one of them whispered open. Thomas Sethy, dressed in a simple white robe arabesqued with green thread, entered the hall. His remaining white hair was hidden beneath a rounded cap of forest-green cloth. The man's visage sparkled. Sam tried to shove aside the thought that Tom burned brightly with the last of his energy. By morning he would be dead.

"Why so pensive, Sam?" Tom asked. There was a teasing grin on the man's face. "Surely by now you've adjusted to lovers dying on you."

Sam looked into the bright blue eyes and remembered the youth he had married in 2660. "You, of all people, should ask that!"

"Just kidding." Tom kissed Sam and took the chair beside him. "I'll have one night bright as a nova, then burn out. Narlo, now, lives like this all the time! How does he do it?"

"With my money!"

Tom broke into a coughing chuckle.

Porcelain-skinned Private walked through the archway from the Grand Salon. His footsteps were a whispering scrape on the tile. Stopping before Sam, he said: "We have completed the investigation you requested."

"And?"

The robot began: "Mister Kittmore spent the last ten years of his life purchasing salvage spacecraft and habitat cylinders and orbiting them out to the Belt. The volume of this activity was—"

"Sammmmy! Not now." Narlo had trotted up beside Sam's chair and stood shaking his finger under Sam's nose. "You promised, no business tonight! The first guests are arriving out front."

Tom rose without the least difficulty, patted Narlo on the head, and walked to a position in the center of the hall, facing the archway to the oval foyer. Sam joined him, but stayed back and to his left; this was Tom's party. The first guests were locals: members of the Assembly, businessmen, and artist friends of Tom. Doc Pulski and his wife arrived. The doctor reassured Sam for ten seconds and headed straight for the buffet. After half an hour of greeting people, Sam had become numb. Then his ears picked up.

"Charles Tell, Councilman of Omaha," announced the majordomo.

The sandy-haired young man greeted Tom with warm words, praising his literary work before passing to greet Sam. "Mayor Phoe, it is a pleasure to meet so famous a man."

"Infamous, I suspect. What brings you to Key West, Councilman?" Without my knowing about it, Sam added in his own mind.

"Trade contracts."

Sam let this unlikely reply pass—Key West and Omaha hadn't been on speaking terms for a hundred years; but he couldn't grill the man at Tom's party. They chatted about sand and sunshine for a moment before the councilman waved to someone and bowed away from him.

"Xian Te of Chengdu."

Sam greeted the plump oriental. After the man had passed into the north hall, Sam waved Private over beside him. "Any record of who that is?"

"Nephew of Su Xian Taua," the robot whispered. "Shall I use the brain link, Mayor?"

Sam shook his head; he didn't want a mouthful of copper spoiling a fortune in exquisite foods.

Why, he wondered, would the nephew of the woman World-News called the Empress of China be in Key West? Recruiting? Her stable of young men was said to rival any sultan's harem. Other than questionable male talent, the island held little for Madame Su.

"Russell Makkle, Under Secretary of State for Charlotte and His Royal Highness Petre, Count of Warsaw."

Petre, a petite man crisply dressed, came frequently to Key West. He was notoriously bisexual, keeping his position by virtue of being the favorite butt of his great uncle's practical jokes. His great uncle was the King of Poland.

But Sam's interest went to the man from Charlotte. He was tall, with curly back hair on the sides of his head and shiny balding spot on top. His handsome face reminded Sam of Gibb's. *Damn! I'm getting hooked on that boy if I see his face on every stranger who walks in my door*, thought Sam.

Tom turned about to face Sam just before the pair reached the reception line. A beaming grin stretched his face. "My God! Sam. I feel like some Corporate Chairman."

Narlo sniffed and broke in: "Well, Sam said to invite all the important tourists. I did. Most of them didn't want to be discovered here either!"

These people were all second-string helpers for important Corporates, cities, or powerful personages, yet that they were in Key West at all might be important to the mysteries that taunted Sam of late. He decided that he couldn't interrogate each guess who came through the door, and so began mentally compiling a litany of questions for a moment when he might corner each later during the party. He shook more hands and listened to the echoing murmur of the crowd, with laughter now added; Tom's guests were beginning to enjoy themselves.

He overheard one already-tipsy woman laugh and remark: ". . . its so quaint here . . . they use human servants!"

An ill-dressed, diminutive man with skin the color and texture of overly tanned leather walked in through the archway. Tom grabbed Sam's hand as if he were frightened—though thrilled amazement was closer to the real emotion. "Jab Ranibi of Patna," called the majordomo. Here came the members of the first string! Though he would giggle and deny it, Jab Ranibi was the planet's most prominent humanist philosopher. The little Indian's name was synonymous with equality and love.

He shook Tom's hand with both of his, not letting go as he spoke: "Thomas Sethy, unless you keep unpublished collections, there is no poem you have ever written that I have not read. They are a boon to my spirit."

Tom effervesced with this praise from Ranibi, and Sam's mouth lifted into the first real smile of the evening to see his lover happy after suffering so long.

"Ah, and Samuel Phoe, I am much overdue at your city. Coming as we do from Glades, your island is like a sunny morning to a coal miner. But that I could stay longer than this night. Alas, in the morning we must be in New Delhi."

Just as Sam began a reply, the next guest was announced: "Alexander of Titan."

Perhaps it was high imagination, but Sam swore that conversation among the late arrivals in the hall ceased. Ranibi eyed the man, Sam noticed, and some of the pert Indian's energy drained visibly from him. Tom greeted the offworlder, then strolled away from the reception line with Ranibi. Narlo departed to inspect the buffet, after first stopping to rebutton an open collar on a servant's jacket. Sam was left to face the smiling Titan. And his size well matched the name.

"I am pleased, Mayor Phoe, to be able to thank you in person for keeping me out of a Glades jail."

"Please, call me 'Sam.' And I'm always happy to thwart Glades."

Adjusting the floor-length, belted white robe he wore, Alexander chuckled. "Well, Sam—my friends call me 'Pip,' a childhood name that stuck—I am truly grateful, so if there's anything I can ever do for you, merely ask."

Pip equaled Sam's height but added to it a hulking frame that made the red-bearded man a dominating figure. Yet he moved with such grace that Sam wondered if he had studied dance. Sam began to feel a tingle inside himself, foretelling that sometime during the evening he would make a pass at the offworlder.

He placed a hand on Pip's back and guided him out of the hall and into the Grand Salon. "Let's see if there are any stars out." With this as an excuse to spirit the fellow outside away from the crowd, they walked through the chatting mass—eyed all the way by Narlo—and out onto the palace terrace. Its grass felt spongy underfoot. He took Pip past the stone gazebo to the wall railing. An armed Fundy watched from twenty feet off.

Pip pointed up, indicating a bright speck of light to the south. "That is not a star." It was one of the newly Glades-owned fortress platforms in geosynchronous orbit.

"Do they trouble you as much as they do me?" asked Sam.

In the light of a gibbous moon Sam watched a grin flick the man's rather thick lips. "Make good targets for a trap shoot."

The sea was still tonight, as if it held its breath.

"There's danger in the air. I can smell it, and I can see it in the faces of our out-of-town guests. Please understand, Pip, that I must ask you. Why are you here?"

"I like boys."

Sam let out a snort. "Why do I have trouble believing that?"

Pip placed a hand on the back of Sam's neck and massaged lightly. "Probably because I'm a lousy liar! In fact, I have a wife and three children, at home."

"Titan?"

"At home. You no doubt know there was a lengthy rebellion, as the Corporates called it, in the Belt and beyond. That's over now. Somebody—namely, me—has to reestablish trade agreements."

In Key West! thought Sam. Well then, we are a pariah city with firm connections to no one.

Music from the small orchestra Narlo had hired drifted out to them, as did the crash of someone's glass shattering on marble. A mild salt breeze quickly pushed these sounds away again. Sam looked at the man's ruddy face; an aspect of it reminded him of someone else—who he couldn't remember.

"The cybe-war tournaments begin on the twenty-fifth. Would you join me in opening them—I have the best seat in the stadium." Sam had a lot more questions. That would be an excellent place to ask them.

Pip nodded. "Sounds like fun. Say, I have a psych show to put on. I'd better check the equipment."

"It's set up in the Music Room. What's the show about?" Sam asked this as they recrossed the terrace, moving toward the triple arches into the Grand Salon.

A mischievous grin crossed the man's face. "Living in the Belt, deep space construction and the like. But if you want a really good show, keep part of your attention on the out-of-town guests."

Now, Sam was sure. All of the important people at Tom's party were present at Alexander of Titan's bidding. And Sam began to suspect that there was more involved than resuming crossing shipments of rare minerals and neuronet cells.

The murmuring of guests in the Music Room sputtered out when Pip stood. The man's size commanded respect while his deep and melodious voice seduced everyone's attention. "From Titan, I bring this psychic work by one of our most gifted artists. It expresses the hopes and the determination of your cousins who reside in Earth's night sky. It is entitled *A Dream in Space*."

As Pip sat down between Sam and Tom, the room lighting faded slightly. A single musical note sounded, but without reverberation or echo; it was struck inside Sam's brain. The Music Room jarred and twisted away into a black hole, leaving nothing in his visual field. Sam's head spun.

The void was suddenly pricked by hundreds of points of light—stars. A lone figure clad in a light space suit floated by and waved. A boy's—or a girl's—grin shone through the clear visor.

The music rose and became strident.

The boy floated up to an ovoid vehicle the size of *Whelp* and entered a yellow-glowing hatchway. As Sam watched the shuttle, it sped out of view until the projection altered to included a spaceship at least as large as Whitehead Palace and the shape of a cucumber. A dilating viewport opened to reveal the same boy, tiny in scale now, waving to them as the craft began to move and thus shift from Sam's perspective.

The background color altered from black to silvery gray. The spaceship traveled across this scene for a minute as the music took on a deeper and somewhat menacing tone. Then, Sam felt his muscles tighten.

In bright green, emblazoned on the shiny background was a giant design: a five-pointed star topped by a castle. *Starcastle*!

Perspective shot backward. The spaceship into which the boy had taken his shuttle became a speck beside the hull of a starship so vast that Key West could have been stowed inside with room to spare! A tuna swimming beside a whale.

But now background for the huge starship had become metallic gray.

The psych show's perspective retreated. As large as the starship was, the object behind dwarfed it. An immense cylinder—and a second one appeared in the distance—slowly turned against a backdrop of faint stars. The unbelievably giant starship became as a pencil to a torpedo. If the cylinder was an inch, it was fifty miles long!

Sam forced aching lungs to take in a breath again.

The view faded to black.

Harplike music drifted into the void; with each note a few pixels of light shone. After several bars, Sam could "see" blades of grass and wind-tossed brown needles around a resin-dripping tree trunk. Robins chirped and flew in and out of the bosky scene. The viewpoint expanded, encompassing a grove of young pines and a small brook gurgling over rounded stones. Butterflies teased the air. The picture expanded again to include an entire forest—as seen from the air—perhaps a mile wide and sandwiched between vast areas of wheatlike golden grass. But this place curved.

Ever so gently just at the horizon, the grasses rose toward

the sky, visually disappearing into layered slate-gray rain clouds. The brook joined a small river, which in turn emptied into a sparkling lake that could float Key West, Sugarloaf, and Cudjoe. He felt a damp breeze off its surface. Sam had seen pictures of space habitat cylinders, whose slow spin-induced "gravity" allowed people to build on its curving inside walls—not this size! The habitat he viewed in Pip's dreamworld could be ten or fifteen miles wide and who knew how long?

The view altered again by turning forty-five degrees.

He now looked the length of the cylinder. In the distance, obscured by a white mist, rose a dozen turquoise towers, sparkling in a yellow glow that came from a bright area of the "sky" above, which appeared to run the length of the cylinder. Here was a fairy castle in some other universe.

On a low hill with the vast city as background, the same boy waved to Sam, a smile lighting his freckled face, the wind tossing his sandy hair.

Using his own computer link, Sam broke his connection with the psychic projector. The hushed Music Room returned, along with the odor of strained perfume and cologne. As Pip had suggested, Sam surveyed the assembled guests. Tom, beside him, was clearly elated by what his mind saw. Along the curving wall, half-a-dozen chairs away, Charles Tell and Russell Makkle sat together, looking pale and drawn. Makkle trembled. Beyond them, Jab Ranibi, hands folded over his chest, glowed with a beatific smile. Across the circular room, Sam spotted Xian Te grinning and nodding his head.

A gasp filled the chamber.

Sam allowed the psychic projection to reenter his mind. Now, the viewpoint rested above the green-glowing curve of a planetary surface. Three of the giant starships orbited by. Were they above Venus—or Earth? Slowly, a whitish sun inched up the horizon. It was too small. Sam felt a gasp jerk from his own throat. A second, dimly reddish sun twice the size of the first caused the planet below to tinge purple. They dreamed of other star systems!

A shiver passed along Sam's body. He shook.

The warmth of a big hand touched his arm and broke the projected image. Pip looked into Sam's eyes and a wide smile flashed perfect teeth.

A complex of thoughts confused Sam's mind: Had he beheld a dream based on the Starcastle myth? Had he been shown a ruse in light designed to intimidate the Corporates and win concessions from them? Or had Pip revealed simple fact?

11

"La, Child! But this is gonna be one busy day." Harsho waved a hand at the streams of people pouring into the stadium. He returned his attention to the automatic dispenser system control panel, which displayed two perverse red lights. After typing in several sets of coded instruction and receiving zero results, he shrugged. He turned to Chip. "Chip honey, if this thing goes the rest of the way to Never-Never Land come get me. I'll have to dig into it."

Gibb watched Harsho duck out one end of the concession stand and enter a tunnel that would lead him around the oval stadium and up to the VIP box. His attention wandered out to the tiers of seats curving under a faint blue glow from the transparent dome. They were packed with people whose pulsating roar reminded Gibb of the ocean that surrounded the city. It made him shake nervously. He had spent too many years in quiet forests.

A cheer nearly split the dome. The masses surged to their feet.

At the opening of the VIP box a white-haired man appeared accompanied by a huge fellow with hair the color of autumn: Lord Sam and Alexander of Titan—Pip. Both men waved to the crowd.

A powerfully voiced heckler in the crowd yelled: "Nice

catch, Sam! When's the wedding?" The mayor shrugged and hunched his shoulders in a who-me? gesture, which brought a round of laughter and cheers from the spectators.

Gibb confessed to himself that Lord Sam's failure to return his message had hurt. But then he was busy, Gibb guessed. Likely Lord Sam already knew what he had wanted to tell him. But Gibb had wondered at the mayor's attending games two days after the death of his lover, Thomas. Harsho had explained that a man's final party limited most people's need for long shows of grief. The mayor's household had held a quiet funeral yesterday, a black ribbon still flew from most flagpoles, and beyond that, any remaining grief lay inside individual hearts. Gibb tried to understand, but would always think of Kao and fail miserably.

He turned back to Chip, who wore a baggy turquoise shirt open to the navel and white shorts three sizes too tight. They made the boy look as if he had a cock the size of an oak limb! "Aren't those uncomfortable?" he asked, pointing to the shorts.

"Yeah, but a guy's gotta advertise. Three months and three days left! You interested?"

Gibb blushed. "My heart's already taken."

"God, not Harsh! He can't handle what he's got!"

But Gibb bobbed his head toward the VIP box and watched a look of dismay cross Chip's face.

"I know he saved you and all that, but. . . . You been with him, ever?"

Gibb nodded.

"Wow! Yeah, but they say he won't touch an islander since his blow-up with Kenton White—soured him." Chip stopped punching in orders and lightly touched Gibb's arm, running a finger along the biceps. "Good luck. If you miss, I wouldn't mind being second choice to Sam Phoe."

Laughing, he bent forward and kissed Chip on the cheek, then pointed at a wild flashing of neglected red lights on the control panel.

A bar of music began and stillness washed the stadium. The rustle of thousands of people standing spilled from the tiers. A slow and melodious hymn began; its words seemed familiar to Gibb, then he remembered: *Secret Lover*, the song Dawn had sung in the church. It was the anthem for Key West, he realized. A deafening cheer ended the hymn.

An odor of freshly popped and buttered corn wafted over the concession stand, making Gibb's mouth water. An ear-splitting yell from thousands of throats rent the air. When this and its echoes died down, a ringing hiss remained.

The PA called out: "Programmed by the Turings—The Silver Bullets!"

At one end of the open area below, a dozen silver, torpedo-shaped objects floated twenty feet off the grass flooring, light glinting from razor-edged fins that ran from a pointed front to a wider rear. Their metal surfaces appeared to ripple, something he wouldn't have believed had he not seen how Lord Sam's flying craft could change shape. Each, Gibb judged, was about five feet long. In a three-dimensional diamond formation, they glided around the stadium.

"Do people fly those?" Gibb asked excitedly.

"Naw. Cybermissiles. Programmed by the various frats—this match, the Turings and Queens."

The announcer droned again as a flight of sparkling gold missiles rose from a wide hatch in the arena floor: "The reigning champs! Programmed by the Queens." A wave of boos and cat-calls filled the stadium. "The Honey Bees!" These let out a sharp buzz as they exploded upward into the open vastness of the stadium.

"Why do they boo the Queens' team?" asked Gibb.

Chip came closer to him and stretched up to place an arm about his shoulders. The boy's warmth sent an unwanted surge of need through Gibb's body. "Well. I'm not sure just yet. It's either because Queens members sell their ass. Or it's how much money they make at it."

An explosion of giggles erupted from the boys working

the drink-filling machines when a feed line came loose and coated one red-haired youth with greenish syrup. Chip rushed over and squeezed the tube back over its nozzle, blowing hair out of his eyes and glowering at the help as he did so. After washing his hands, he returned to Gibb's side. "I gotta go see Harsh. This damn thing's fallin' apart."

Gibb watched him leave and take the same route up to the higher tiers and the stand beside the VIP box, admiring the wiggle of his well-outlined, cute ass as he trotted away. He liked Chip and wondered if a mental pursuit of Mayor Phoe was more dream than reality. Why not settle down with Chip? Because, I'm not in love with Chip, he reminded himself. I'm in love with Lord Sam!

The ringing hiss doubled volume. Gibb looked out in time to see one of the golden cybermissiles spin downward, dart below the silvers, and loop up into their midst. Its blade-like fins elongated, then scraped and tore into two of the silver machines. They spun out of control, smashing into the arena floor with a crunching thud.

Yelling and cheering tore at the stadium walls.

But now the other members of both teams spun wide away from each other and looked to engage an enemy. The open air sparkled and flashed with their maneuvers. A Turings' missile bunted upward into the fins of a Queens, knocking off its tail and sending it into a fatal downward spin. More cheers—louder. Two silver cybermissiles creased a golden one between them, but failed to disable it.

Gibb felt his heart pound with excitement as he watched, unable to force his attention back to business. When he did tear his gaze away, he felt embarrassed, for the younger boys worked like mad to fill orders, not the least distracted. Some example he was!

A massive gasping of breath tore from the crowd. A booming crash followed. Gibb refused to turn around. He would attend to business. But so much panicked dismay had stopped the boys' work. They rushed to the counter and gaped up. Gibb too looked. His heart jumped.

All of the missiles had been brought to the arena floor. But an area of the upper stands was a ruin of twisted metal and gaping hole. A thin smoke arose from the point where one of the golden missiles had dived clear through the VIP box!

The PA shouted: "There is no danger. Remain calm. But, please, leave the stadium at once by your assigned exits!"

Gibb sprinted out of the concession stand. He moved along a row of seats, dodging people or shoving between them until he reached the arch into the service corridor. A dim tunnel led him past dozens of cartlike servos, halted in their routine of delivering sodas and popcorn, and to an elevator. Its slow rise nearly drove him to distraction. And when it opened, fifty feet or so from the VIP box, a Fundy stood blocking his path.

He tried to rush past the giant. A massive hand on his chest stopped the effort cold. Tears blinded Gibb. "Lord Sam! I have to see, Lord Sam!"

The guard shook him hard. "No! We attend to Samuel. Are you one of the concessionaires?"

Gibb nodded.

"You had best assist your coworkers. The medics are on their way, but—"

He looked about, then broke free of the man and darted toward a section of mangled planking where the upper control area for Harsho's business had been. Before him he could see what had happened: a malfunctioning missile had punched a wide hole through one side of the VIP box, out the other, and into the concession stand. The missile had rammed the wooden counter, shattering it into spikes. Several empty seats bristled with pieces of wood. Luckily, the section had been unoccupied.

A fear he had not known since the beach where Lord Sam rescued him poured over Gibb, slowing his pace. He was afraid of what he would find among the rubble. Workers moved about the rear, shooting white vapor at flicks of fire. Beneath one large plank, he could see Harsho watching him—he was okay!

Gibb ran forward, then froze. The thing under the planking wasn't Harsho. It was Harsho's severed head.

Acid filled his mouth. A sharp pain in his knees told him he had dropped to the floor. His breakfast shot out of him onto the carpet. A wrenching sob tore at him. His mind began to pass into a gray fog of despair.

"Gibb."

He stirred at the weak voice calling his name, rose unsteadily, and followed a sound of coughing to the side of a battered mixing machine. Chip's face smiled up at him. Blood dribbled out the corner of his mouth and down a pale cheek. The boy's skin had lost its rosy color. Gibb rushed to his side and started to lift him. He stopped. A shard of wood that had been polished oak counter top was sticking from his side, angled up under the boy's ribs.

"Don't move!" he shouted as Chip made an effort to shift himself despite a grimace of pain. Blood now leaked from the boy's nose, and caused him to cough, then wince.

"Gibb. I'm not gonna make it to legal, am I?"

"Sure you will!" But Gibb's words sounded atop another sob, negating their truth.

"Glad I cheated once. Wish it had been with you. Muscles. . . ."

The boy's eyes stopped focusing and stared at him, lifeless. The once rebellious topknot stood proudly upward. Gibb felt for a pulse, but found none.

He stayed there with Chip's head in his lap, thinking of Kao and of this boy, who he would never know better, until a medic pulled him off. A black emotional fog swirled about and closed over him.

12

"Light." The ceiling illumination rose. Doc Pulski removed the shadows to examine Pip. Sam's bedroom had ample windows, yet an approaching storm, which flickered lightning flashes into the room from time to time, cast a pall over everything. He ran a portable scanner across every inch of the naked man. "He will be all right. Just a mild concussion. Was it an accident, Mayor?"

Sam grunted and shrugged.

The doctor placed a shiny cap on Pip's head and set a dial on its front. "That'll cool him down a little, ease the headache when he wakes up." Doc rose and turned toward Sam. "I'm working on a drug to balance your aging, so you won't experience surges of regional deterioration. It will take another week or two."

If he lasted that long! Sam thought about the shortness of breath he had experienced after running from the stadium, but said, "Thanks, Doc. It's been better for a few days now."

He watched the tall man depart, trying, as he said, to reach home before the sky broke. When Sam sat down on the edge of the giant poster bed, a mild stab of pain reminded him that he had his own set of bruises from the aberrant cybermissile. He eyed Pip for a minute before pulling up the silk sheet. His frame and musculature were massive, but well proportioned.

Pip's cock looked a major threat even soft. The man's skin had a ruddy glow and smoothness that demanded touching. The palm of Sam's hand rubbed across his chest between rosy nipples and through a light bushing of curly red hair. The action brought a tingle to his own body. Something about the man haunted him.

Lightning flashed into the room again as a gust of wind tore at the gauze drapes over the ocean-facing windows. Loud and rolling thunder followed.

Sam finished pulling up the sheet and stood. He grabbed the robe he wore tight about him as he walked to the window and stepped out onto the hemicircle of balcony. He blinked into a roaring and chill wind. A lightning-veined wall of black approached Key West. The sea churned with a moving geology of liquid white mountains. There would be no touring ships docking today. Tiny drops of rain stung his face. That was as much warning as nature gave, so he retraced his steps into the bedroom and told the computer to seal his suite. All the windows hummed, slid down, and clicked into place.

Moving through double doors, he entered the bewickered morning room, then turned into the den. Here, he flopped down behind his slant-topped desk. He placed his thumb on the corner and a symbol pad appeared beside his hand. He keyed for Uriel Fordac.

A minute passed with Sam drumming an index finger on the smooth surface. A burst of light appeared before him and twisted into focus as the Fundy Captain. "Hail, Samuel!"

"Well?"

The man lowered his wrap, revealing a bearded face with clenched, square jaw. "Someone altered the cybermissile's macroinstructions. We are questioning members of the Queens' programming team—"

"Gently, I hope."

"Aye, Samuel. The missiles had been sealed away day before yesterday. The sabotage was likely done before then, though we can't be certain."

That didn't answer the biggest question in Sam's mind: precisely who was the target? The Glades Secret Police might be after him for kicking their agents off the island . . . or it could be that whatever Pip did in Key West was making someone very nervous. If assassination failed, what came next?

"Captain, how far out are our explosive mines?"

The Fundy looked down at the computer terminal on his wrist before he answered. "Two concentric circles at half a mile and one mile. Another hundred sea-to-air missile mines remain in stowage."

The chair creaked as Sam leaned back. In all the years he had been mayor, he had never actually had to defend the city, though once or twice war came uncomfortably close. Now, luckily, he had *Bitch in Heat*, who equaled twenty air floaters and could sink most any ship afloat.

"Have the computers work out an optimum pattern using all our mines for defending the island against a siege. Send me an inventory of our weaponry. Oh, and Uriel, please thank the guardsman who knocked us out of the missile's path." He still hurt from that flying tackle, but he was alive.

The Fundy flashed a rare smile. "The guard will be pleased by your praise. Hail, Samuel." The image vanished.

Sam released a long sigh, then called up from data storage his project evaluating connections between the mythical Starcastle and Auggy Kittmore that the twin robots, Private and Sergeant, had completed. Paragraphs and equations flashed onto the desk surface. They said much, and nothing: pure speculation.

Over a ten-year period a hundred and sixty years ago, Kittmore had bought junked ships, orbiting them into deep space. All of it piled together, melted down, and refabricated might build one ship with a length of three miles.

"Whale piss! Fantasy!" And Pip must be playing on it, whatever actually happened to the fleet sent by the Corporate Council to quell the Belt rebellion. Create doubt and fear. Excellent strategy. But suddenly Sam thought about Hacker reproducing himself, which in turn brought to mind Areal Silvas and his Von Neumann digging machines, which duplicated themselves when they had taken in enough raw material.

Sam leaned forward and began tapping new questions. What if Auggy had begun with Von Neumann, or self-reproducing, robot construction machines? Hacker's behavior proved that this could be done at the highest level of robotics. What if all those scrapped ships and microworlds had been converted to more Von Neumann machines? How large of an industrial base could be built? Now have the computer factor-in the constraints of distance in the Belt and outer system, and. . . .

The tabletop flashed a question at him: *Time frame?*

It surprised Sam that his fingers shook as he entered the number of years he estimated: *160.*

More numbers and equations flowed in green light across the desk surface.

After staring at the hypothesis for several minutes, he rose from the chair, shaking the length of his body. He was uncertain whether it was fear or excitement that accompanied his speculations. He walked back out to the dimly lighted morning room, and stood staring at the sheets of rain slashing his windows. It was three in the afternoon, but looked like midnight.

"Fantasy!"

How could those figures be correct? Humans, in all their history, had never carried off a project of such size. One super-smart faggot could do it? No way! But then, his obedient machines would have carried it out. Still, if one tenth of what the equations indicated was correct, the Corporate Council's war-canoe navy was fighting a battle with the US Sixth Fleet! It wouldn't be a war; it would be a one-sided exercise in patience and restraint.

His energy drained, Sam moved slowly into the bedroom. Again he looked at the handsome man lying on his wide bed.

Key West, 2720 A.D.

Who was he? The Ambassador from Starcastle? An admiral trying to decide which cities to burn away should the need arise? He certainly had the bearing of a military man. If either side blinked, Key West might be scraped from the face of the planet.

"You will stare the skin off of me, Sam." The man was awake and grinning up at him.

"They missed us. I brought you here when I became unsure exactly who the assassins were after. Whitehead Palace is the most secure place on the island."

"It was an assassination attempt then?" Pip asked. A frown wrinkled his forehead.

Sam nodded.

A grin returned to Pip's mouth. "How safe am I here?"

He returned the man's grin. "As safe as you want to be, Pip. Let me ask you a question. Do your people exclude gays?" Sam had to ferret out some idea of the moral climate of the change that swept so near the planet.

Pip's face flushed and twisted to anger before resuming a neutral stance. His answer boomed from the walls: "We find no cause to exclude anyone! Earth is the core of our species, Sam, and its rotting stench reaches to the stars!"

He seemed embarrassed by his angry-preacher's tone. His voice softened. "Here you of Earth sit, dead still; you have sat dead still for four hundred years, Sam. In the Belt we never stop moving. We never stop needing new ideas, new ways of doing things—we banish no one."

"But I speak of sexual love, not disagreements in physics theory," Sam reminded.

A sharp crack of thunder shook the building.

The man's caution threw up a wall: "Well, I'm just a trade ambassador. But in deep space people must work together, which requires that our laws make sense. At the Belt and outer systems, loving someone of your same sex is no big deal. Take my word for it."

Sam had trouble lifting his gaze from a mountain rising in the sheets halfway down the bed. Sight of it started him shaking again. As he turned to go, he said: "Well, rest till tomorrow. I'll have a tray of food sent up in case you're hungry later."

"Sam. I'm something of a stallion in heat. . . . I mean I'm not too versatile in bed." He patted the sheets beside him.

Sam felt his heart begin to pound. A rush of blood made him dizzy. "You don't have to prove what you said. I believe you."

Pip's grin became lopsided. "Look. I'm horny as hell and too tired, lazy, and injured to try and woo a female bedmate. Come here!"

Sam sat on the edge of the bed. He closed his eyes as Pip's wide hand moved inside the robe and traced a slow route across his chest. He felt an eager twitching in his ass. Between tremors, Sam said, "You implying I'm easily had?"

"Are you?"

"Yes." The thought that he was second choice after some tavern wench stayed in Sam's mind three nanoseconds.

Pip awakened to a flood of moonlight over his face. He glanced at a band of faint green light on the wall that gave time and temperature: 2 A.M. and chilly. He shifted across the soothing sheets. The bed swayed slightly as he left it; Sam moaned, but didn't wake. Pip tossed on his pants and tunic, then bent over the bed and kissed Sam on the cheek. Pip had never thought love making with another man would be that enjoyable or how much passion expanded versatility; he had learned something new.

His head throbbed when he rose too fast from the kiss.

But as he looked down at the young face with its topping of ancient hair, Pip realized that this man had likely known Auggy Kittmore. If only he could talk to Sam about the man. Perhaps Sam would know what person was meant by Auggy's reference to "the man of Key West." His mother had demanded two things of him before he began this project: logical compassion and the name of the man so vaguely referred to by her father.

Now, he would have trouble providing her with either! Pip traveled across the silver-coated room and out onto an enclosed veranda. Its windows stood open and a cool breeze delivered a rich vegetal odor from the rain-soaked gardens below.

Somewhere, he knew, Sam would have a comm room that could provide him a link with his ship. He had talked and negotiated as reason allowed. Why give the Corporates a second chance to make him a hostage? If what he had told their underlings didn't sufficiently impress the great businesses and city-states, then he must turn the matter over to someone else's logical compassion. And how much of that rare commodity did Admiral Yeasavich possess? But, regardless, the responsibility for what happened next would always be his. A sobering thought.

A brown den with clear desk turned on its lighting when Pip entered. Here was the comm room.

He sat down in a complaining chair behind the desk and examined its controls. They appeared unguarded. Wishing a channel out, he touched one of the switches that should gain him a line. A holo image flashed into the room; Pip jumped, thinking he had called one of Sam's Fundies. No, someone had left a memory cube in the machine. Then he looked at the glowing figure before him.

The figure spoke. Pip listened intensely to every word, and with each one, his mouth fell further open. At last the message stopped, and the ghost vanished.

"Well, now I know who Auggy meant by 'the man of Key West.' And I just slept with him."

One thing became instantly clear: There was no longer time for a message and more waiting. He must leave Key West and the planet—now. Opening his mental computer link, Pip

sent out a call to one of Sam Phoe's cyberbrain robots.
THIS IS SERGEANT.

A twinge of anguish touched Pip for what he must do, but his choices were limited. Sam wouldn't understand, and it would hurt him. But his submarine was the only vehicle that could get Pip under Corporate spotter craft to where he had left his shuttle, beneath thirty feet of water off Andros Island. *Have* Bitch in Heat *readied. I must leave Key West immediately.*
YES, MASTER KITTMORE.

Later, when he had the time, Pip would sort out the emotions evoked from having made love to his own grandfather.

13

Little by little over an hour or two, Gibb's awareness returned from an unending chain of daymares. He had no idea what time it was or how long he had been wandering. It was dark. But he had a vague memory of passing the afternoon and night of the day Harsho and Chip died curled into a ball beneath a bush in the park. He had been rained on, but hadn't cared. Now at least he sat on a bench, near a spur of lake. Its waters glowed blood red from reflections of a light-show overhead.

I'm a curse, he thought. *Everyone I care about dies!*

A sob shook him as he buried his head in his hands. Had he once said to Harsho how much he liked the man? Couldn't he have kissed Chip's lips once, just to say 'I like you'? What would happen to the household? Did Harsho's family want his children?

The bench creaked. Gibb felt a soft hand on his shoulder. He looked up into green eyes given a bluish tint by the hellish glow.

"You hide better than anyone on the island. I've been looking a day and a half," said Dawn.

Gibb sat up and allowed his head to loll about. The kinks hurt. His nose ran from the previous night's chill, so he wiped at it with his sleeve. "They think I jinxed the missile?"

She expelled a warm laugh. "We Fundies take great pride in knowing what goes on here, and where folks are. So, when the mayor asked if you had been hurt—"

"Lord Sam is alive!" A flood of joy shoved back an intractable misery.

"—we went looking for you. You hide good!"

Dawn scooted closer to him. With a hesitation that he felt as several light, preliminary touches she began massaging the back of his neck. It sent chills up and down his spine.

"Death is never easy," Dawn said with a far-away tone to her voice, "especially when it must come to good and innocent persons. But death's best when sudden. With no time for thought."

"How many died?"

"Your sponsor, one of his junior managers—Chip Reed—and four people to the far side of the VIP box. Sudden." She shifted her hand to his right shoulder and pulled him closer to her. "I can see it, Gibb. Death." She allowed her words to ferment for a few minutes. "My people are going to die. And I can see it!"

He turned his face toward hers. Red tears glistened down smooth cheeks. "You can see the future that clearly? Warn them."

Dawn shook her head. "When the time comes, I will. And they will stubbornly refuse to hear my words. They will do as they have always done. This time it will kill them."

The young woman's warm touch and the fact that she confided such important matters to his ear gave Gibb's spirit a desperately needed lift. He reached an arm about her waist and felt her tremble. With but a second's hesitation, Gibb leaned over and kissed Dawn. Her ravenous response shocked him. Her tongue sought his while needful arms surrounded his body. Such powerful desire evoked a masculine reflex buried deep inside Gibb's nature.

She pulled him up from the bench and over to a spread of

grass that lay beneath weeping limbs. Her hands were inside his shirt, running softly and warmly over his back. Feeling his crotch, she found the erection she hoped for and began stripping her own clothing. Not waiting for Gibb to undress fully, Dawn drew him down to the cool grass with her.

She made love to him in a frantic way, as if a thousand years of ghosts chased her. Gibb felt less a part of it than he wanted to be; nevertheless, he responded with youthful but inept gusto to his first sexual encounter with a female.

Afterward, a postmating glow buoyed him and pushed away the low clouds of his gloom.

A crunching sound on the path cut into Gibb's mellowness. A giant dressed in white shoved aside the low-hanging branches and peered down at the couple. Rage chased dismay across his face. The Fundy drew his sidearm.

"Blasphemer!"

Gibb's heart jumped. He leaped up. Forgetting any effort at dressing, he sprinted from under the lone tree, dashed naked through open lawn, and darted into a grove of young pines. Fallen cones abused his feet. He heard shouting behind him. Some projectile thudded through the branches six inches above his hair. Ducking, Gibb kept running, his bare skin being whipped by every tree branch and thorn bush he passed.

To where!

After two hundred yards, he slowed and listened for pursuit. Nothing but crickets and party noises from Duval Street. But in the flickering red glow he spotted a line of white shapes moving quietly through the distant trees. They were after him! There was no appeal for what they would do when they got their hands around his throat—if it wasn't his balls they went for first! He had spent a week's vacation in Key West and was once again being kill-hunted. Gibb moaned and headed away from the meticulous search.

Another hundred yards farther on he spotted the southern archway out of the park. That would be watched. His eyes darted along the ten-foot-high border wall—smooth and unclimbable. "This way!" a Fundy too near at hand shouted to his fellows. Gibb took deep breaths and repressed panic. He thought of turning east toward the museum complex with its climbable guttering, but white figures to that direction said he would never make it. A chill of fear ran through him.

"I'm worm food." He wondered if they would simply cut his throat or torture him first.

Then he spotted a trash drum. He rushed for it, took off the lid, and jumped into sticky papers and the odor of decaying apple cores. Like a mole, Gibb dug down till he scraped bottom, placing two feet of souring waste over him. One thing he knew about his hiding place made him nervous: periodically, the bottom opened and all the garbage was sucked into underground compacters. If he stayed too long, the city's automatic waste system would do the Fundy's job for them. What if they flushed the system to be sure no one hid in it!

He waited. And waited, listening to his own confined breathing, regretting the fetid air he consumed. Time lost meaning. At one point someone removed the drum's lid and tossed something in. Gibb held his breath and prayed to every god whose name he could remember. They clanked the cover back on.

Later, vibrations shook the container. He panicked. His fingers groped about, searching for any hold before he was sucked away to his death. Inside, the drum was perfectly smooth. He had to chance the outside.

Just as he burst up through the trash, forcing off the lid and grabbing the rim, the bottom slid away. With a whoosh the contents vanished. He quickly pulled himself out of the container and looked around.

No one.

Gibb licked salty blood from his left palm; the drum rim had been sharper than he thought. His hand had already begun to ache. How much time had passed? At least three hours, he guessed.

Realizing what he must do, Gibb again edged toward the southern gate. If the Fundies would kill him on sight, only one man might prevent it—Lord Sam. Remembering the slippery rocks on the outside of the seawall, Gibb reasoned that it was equally likely that he would die trying to reach the man he loved as it was that the Fundies would get him. He had to try.

Only stillness awaited him at the gate. The hour must be later than he thought, for even Casa Marina Avenue was empty of revelers. He darted across the street, stopping at the side of a giant tree that shaded a multiporched home. Nothing moved to pursue him. Slowly, stepping carefully, more to prevent cuts from the sharp gravel than to be silent, Gibb followed the side of the old house to its rear alley. This ran between the homes along Casa Marina and the massive gray seawall. It groaned in a brisk wind, a grabbing wind that would make what he had to do all the deadlier.

The alley came out at one corner of the Church of the Secret Lover. Now, he knew exactly where he was. Ghostly moonlight and whistling air occupied the overlook plaza. Gibb ran along the stone balustrade until the statue of The Colonel hid him from view. Bending over the railing, he spotted the first jutting block on the route to Whitehead Palace. It was about ten feet below; a churning of silver and green water waited another thirty feet below for his first misstep.

Edging over the balustrade, he allowed himself to slide down the sloping and uneven stone and concrete until his feet rested atop the misaligned block. His buttocks and shoulders burned from abrasions.

Wind whipped his hair and froze his naked body.

The next stone appeared much farther away than it had from above. It was also narrower. If he went into the water, there was no way back up. And he couldn't swim. Taking in several deep breaths first, Gibb leaped the distance, grabbing a short section of old pipe embedded in the concrete to steady himself. Pain shot through his hand. He had forgotten his wounded palm. Still, he made it. But how many dozens more such jumps would it take?

The next six blocks took him below the blank-walled Fundy Barracks. When the salt wind didn't drown the sound out, low and sad hymns drifted down to him.

Crashing waves shot cold spray up at him. Twice, slippery surfaces nearly threw him off the wall.

After crossing below the barracks, the real game began. The route he needed to travel shot upward forty more feet above wave-tortured, sharp rocks. Now he worked nearly numb toes into wide cracks and ascended a foot or two whenever the layered flaws came close enough. His fingers ached and bled so profusely that at one tight move he nearly lost his hold to the slipperiness of his grip. When he rounded the corner of the government complex, Gibb discovered he had made one fatal mental error.

He had assumed that the seawall surfaces from the overlook all the way to Whitehead were the same: rough and climbable. But all seventy vertical feet of the palace's seawall shone and flashed in the moonlight. It was polished white marble. Any crack present might have yielded to the width of a blade of grass, or maybe not.

Fingers and toes unfeeling, Gibb clung to the last jutting block on his road, still forty feet from where he needed to be. A feeling of guilt overwhelmed him. Onalsey was dead, Kao was dead, Chip and Harsho were dead—why did he so selfishly cling to life? He cried.

An unexplainable inner glow warmed his spirit. The guilt relented.

Then he cursed himself for stupidity and began a climb toward the Assembly Building roof. He would come at Whitehead Spit from above! Thanks to a huggable storm gutter, he reached the brown-tile roof with ease. All of Key West lay before him, Duval Street glittering even at this late hour. To his right, the flat-roofed barracks loomed, silent now. Twin plazas, lighted by flickering gas torches, stepped their way up to the building on whose roof he stood. But Gibb's attention quickly riveted to the distant, massive building high on a hill to his left: Whitehead Palace.

Moving to the edge of the roof, Gibb spotted another drain pipe that descended to where he wanted to go. With only minor friction burns, he reached the park that surrounded the palace and began a trot up the hill. Why, he wondered, weren't there guards about? A distant and vaguely familiar ringing hiss answered his question.

"Oh, shit!"

Two glowing spots of light floated his way. Cybermissiles! Once already tonight he had managed to evade what chased him by diving into things, but nothing presented itself but a black-looking pond spotted with water lily pads. He jumped in.

Below a layer of slime he found clear, cold water. He went to the bottom and dug his feet into a fine mud. Could they detect him here? Did they work under water? He floated in the darkness afraid even to release useless air, which caused his lungs to ache, for fear of alerting the robot destroyers. Gibb thought about Sam Phoe so that he felt less the pressure and pain of not breathing. For one night in the man's arms, he would give up his life and consider it fully lived—even at eighteen.

Something cold and snakelike slithered across his leg. He panicked.

Without thought of the consequences, Gibb shot to the surface and gasped in a month's supply of sweet air. Nothing but his wheezing sounded in the night. He waded out of the water, washing the ooze from between his toes as he did so. Pulling a section of plant off his head, he said: "Cybermissiles aren't so bright after all."

A high-pitched voice came from behind him. "May we help you?"

Gibb spun around. Two tubular machines hung by metal tentacles from the branches of an oak that overhung the pond. The nose of one shined a beam of red light onto his chest. No move he made would be fast enough to prevent the robot from turning up the power and burning a hole clear through him. He stood and trembled.

"I'm Gibb. I have come to see Lord Sam."

The second cybermissile flashed white light across his body. "Why do you enter the grounds in this manner?" asked the machine that kept the coin-sized circle over his heart.

If I lie, they'll know it, Gibb thought, realizing how thoroughly the things might be sensing his body. "I had a run-in with the Fundies, and they want to kill me. Lord Sam will help, I hope."

"Ah, the Fundy Sect, such illogical creatures," said the second missile. "We have tried to convince Samuel that more of our kind can better defend the city. Alas, he does not listen. Then, we are expensive and the Fundies are cheap."

The machine fixed to kill Gibb added, "You are likely correct that Samuel will assist your cause. Unless there are other Gibbs in Key West, it is you he calls for in his sleep."

"That is private!" snapped the other machine as it dropped off the limb, spread newly formed wings, and shot away toward the palace.

"Enter on the far side of Whitehead, through the garden court. Fundies! Hah!" This machine also released its hold and flashed by Gibb's head so close he felt a blast of hot exhaust.

Gibb didn't care. "Sam dreams of me!" he yelled, then ducked down for fear a Fundy might be patrolling the grounds and have heard him.

He quickly crossed the open parkland between the lily pond and the huge stone building. As he passed before it, its tall and shadowed arches reminded Gibb of open mouths ready to swallow—him. Avoiding the front drive, he traversed the two hundred yards of stone front as fast as he could pick a course through the moonlit landscape. At last he reached the far end. A double row of columns provided an opening into an inner courtyard. A jetting fountain produced the only sound. Now where? he wondered.

To his left, a section of covered walkway was lighted with a dull yellow glow. Everywhere else was dark. Gibb took the hint. The walk led to a set of metal doors that slid away as he approached. He entered. But footsteps echoed down the hall toward him. A door to his right popped open. Gibb ducked into a humming collection of wires and pipes. The place smelled of burnt plastic and wet plaster.

By the time he began to have trouble breathing, the door clicked and reopened. He moved down the wide, carpeted passageway again, stopping just past a short hall with a cluster of three doors down it. Beyond, the hall was dark. Here was an elevator. It sang lightly; the car was descending. A plaintive sound drew Gibb's attention.

It was a gurgling moan.

The distraction came from down the side hall. Gibb eyed the still unopened elevator, then decided to have a look. He darted over to the narrow hall, noting that one door stood slightly ajar. It was a small bedroom with single bunk, wooden desk, and toppled bright red chair. Holograms of distant places covered the walls. But in the center of the room, a young man was suspended from the ceiling, hanging by the neck.

The fellow moaned and his body shook slightly. His face was bright red. Gibb righted the chair and jumped up on it, grabbing and lifting the young man to take the strain off his neck. He was heavy. First loosening the tie of bed sheet, Gibb next removed the improvised noose. The fellow coughed and gasped and spit sticky liquid on Gibb's back. Only after he had placed the would-be suicide on the bed did Gibb get a look at his face. Brio!

Standing, Gibb spotted a stray pair of shorts on the floor and put them on—a close enough fit. He eyed a collection of knives and daggers on the wall. Brio gurgled at him; Gibb came closer and sat on the edge of the bed.

He could barely make out Brio's faint whisper: "I didn't know the pain would be so bad—choking, head bursting . . . but you shouldn't have stopped me."

"I know." Gibb remembered when Dawn had nearly killed him because of Brio's trick.

"No you don't. I . . . killed those people in the stadium!" For a minute he could not form words with his swollen tongue. "I let Glades agents down into the storerooms—they. . . ." Brio choked off from tears and damaged vocal cords.

A fury burned inside Gibb.

He rose from the bed and walked slowly to the wall. A fat-bladed dagger found his hand. Revenge was the code of the forest. This man had killed Harsho and Chip. Turning, Gibb walked back to the bed and looked down at a wide-eyed Brio. The youth whimpered.

Gibb took hold of his black hair and jerked Brio's head back. Sheet burns formed an orange stripe across a flushed and bruised throat. He pressed the blade down. It was so sharp that blood flowed from his slightest touch.

Brio said nothing, closed his eyes.

"Shit!" Gibb threw the knife at the desk. It twanged and stuck quivering in the wood.

He moved to beside the desk. On it Brio had stacked a collection of gold and silver coins—a sizable fortune. Gibb flipped through these with his index finger, sending those unwanted clinking or thudding onto the tile floor. A total of seventeen dollars he took, then turned back to Brio.

"My change from the rum drinks." He turned to leave the room, then stopped and again faced Brio. "I've had the strangest damn things I've ever seen help me reach Sam tonight. So, it isn't so odd I help you. Dead, you can't help anybody. Just remember, I hate your guts!" He flipped a tiny silver coin onto the bed beside Brio. "That's for the shorts."

14

Roscoe Thorsel watched his boss pace. Both men waited for a connection with members of the Corporate Council; a computer delay rubbed Sudger's fur the wrong way. Turning his back on the comm area, Thorsel walked to the portion of Sudger's office that cantilevered out to form an oriel on the side of the eighty-story US AgriCorp Building. Tile clicked underfoot. Long, draping vines and potted palms produced a jungle effect and a rich vegetal odor of soil that he liked. Morning sunlight shone in, dampened by filters that allowed a clear view of Glades and Lake Okeechobee far below. The city hugged the lake like a horseshoe, and the water itself sparkled a gray-green light up into his eyes. Slate-colored, anvil-shaped thunderheads gathered to the southeast.

Thorsel stopped in the middle of the jutting room, for beyond, the flooring was transparent. It always made his stomach twitch. He tasted the silence of the place and wished he could return to his farm early. All the towering sophistication of city-states made him nervous; which was why he wanted Key West so badly: it was a low-tech place where a person could still smell the shit.

"We have them, Roscoe."

Thorsel turned his back to the view and reentered Sudger's office. Its carpet massaged his tired feet. The boss stood within a surround of six screens. These had taken on a turquoise glow. One after the other, in random order, they filled with smiling faces. Each nervously mumbled a greeting. The chairman of Solsys was missing. He had been at Mars Colony Seven when the blackout began.

"Jacksen, why has Solsys sealed us out of its data banks?" the CEO of Teledata Worldwide asked Sudger.

Thorsel watched his boss's blank expression, only the further narrowing of thin lips told that the question annoyed him. Before answering, he smoothed back his silvering black hair.

"Too much disinformation has already flowed in over their channels. All that crap about Starcastle! It'll stay blocked until we discover what is really causing this blackout."

At mention of the mythical Starcastle two of the Chairmen blanched, Thorsel noted. No wonder Sudger had succeeded in bullying them at last; they were all scared shitless! They would follow anybody who talked a good line, or just yelled loud enough.

"I can tell you this. We have word that the rebels are using a jamming device to block signals. Within the week, I expect a ship from the Solsys fleet to take up Earth orbit. It will bring the information we need."

Bullshit, Thorsel observed, to himself. The Solsys fleet his boss had ordered sent to quell the rebellion was a year overdue. And for all they knew the bogeyman had eaten every human beyond lunar orbit.

"Some of you have been talking to the rebel ambassador," Sudger continued to the paling of those before him. "He has played on your fears. Exactly how much military force do you think a handful of ragtag Belt miners could have? Don't be fools to trickery! The armed platforms circling this planet make us invulnerable."

This last comment was a subtle reminder that Glades now owned the big guns pointing down everyone's collar. Now,

Thorsel knew he wasn't the brightest man present, but even he understood that if the Belt decided to throw rocks—say, ten miles across and bigger—all the laser platforms together wouldn't help. Earth would never know what hit her.

Roscoe Thorsel had his own idea of what was myth. And of what had the glint of cold blade steel. Now was his one chance to take Key West. Whatever was coming after the Corporates wasn't likely to concern itself with a small town off the end of Florida. If he could take it, he could hold it.

Sudger was still lecturing: "Whoever is supplying food to the Excludeds tribes, I want it stopped! Most of the city-states you control have slackened from the pace of extermination we set. Speed it back up!"

Five years ago, these men would have chewed up Jacksen Sudger and spit out his polished bones, Thorsel reflected while listening to his stomach growl. Twenty flapjacks had been too light a breakfast.

When Thorsel looked back up, the screens were blank. Sudger was pissed in general; now, if Thorsel could redirect that anger slightly. . . . "You know, Jacksen, Key West has been the meeting spot for those visiting the rebel ambassador. Makes you look the fool." Thorsel saw Sudger's eyes narrow; he was on dangerous ground. "How long you gonna let Sam Phoe make a fool of you?"

Jacksen Lear Sudger said nothing. He turned and walked to his black-marble desk and sat down. Such silence made Thorsel shudder inside—had he dared too much?

"No longer, Roscoe. Do what you want with the town. But no one is to leave that Sodom alive. No one!"

She stared out into blackness. Two marble-sized objects, one bluish and much larger than the other whitish one, floated there. Though any screen in any cabin aboard *Augustina Regina* could have displayed a more detailed picture, she wanted to see the real thing. Here at this portal only thick transparsteel and space stood between her and the mother planet. She had never seen Earth. Her mother and her grandmother had never seen Earth. Each day now, she came down here and feasted her eyes upon it.

"When will you know, Admiral?" asked Captain Adelatmont, late of the Corporate fleet. His voice echoed slightly in the vast storage chamber. Uneasily, the man eyed the rows of two-hundred-foot-long shuttle craft suspended above their heads.

Mia Iemasa Yeasavich, High Admiral of Starcastle, ignored the man for several minutes. She was not inclined to free conversation with murderers. It was true that Adelatmont had helped convince many city-state officials to talk with Pip; still, the captain had fired on an unarmed mining colony, killing two thousand people.

"We will know when we know," she replied at last.

The truth was that she feared for Pip. He had been gone too long without sending word. The young man had left Key West in a purloined multicraft, and she had not heard from him since. Why risk going there and talking? If she had had her way!

"Come!"

She spun about, strode from the viewing area, and passed through an airlock into an elevator. Adelatmont scurried after. She could hear the plump man's wheezing.

At level twenty-seven the lift doors opened onto the lower deck of the bridge, a place lined by green-glowing monitor screens attended by dozens of operators whose main function was to monitor the lines of code produced by the ship's self-programming computers. When some sequence appeared out of order, they flagged it for the director level of cyberbrain. All unnecessary, in her opinion. Auggy Kittmore's machines hadn't made an error in living memory.

She clanked softly up a flat-runged ladder to the command area, nodding to the robot, Director Nine, as she passed him. "No word?" Nine shook his head.

The captain didn't follow her into the glass-domed office, and so the admiral had the place to herself. She took a seat behind a flat end of an otherwise round conference table and threw a projection of the Earth-Luna system on the curving wall. A tight place to maneuver! When the time came, she would see whether their ships were positioned where they should be.

A bell rang and Commander Marsha Frost, her lover, walked in. Mia smiled at the younger woman.

"Here we sit," said the admiral, "had I known for how long, I would have brought more yarn!"

An added worry for both women was that their son, Loren, served aboard the *Titan III*, which like all the other ships had been under radio silence for a month. Each captain knew that no shipboard emergency justified a transmission. *Titan III* might be destroyed; she and Marsha wouldn't know.

The bell sounded again as Nine walked into the domed office. The robot offered Admiral Yeasavich a tiny cube. "Just decoded—from the Emperor."

Mia accepted it with her eyes closed. Now, we shall know, she thought. "Call the flag officers and Captain Mutra."

Within ten minutes Captain Andrew Mutra of the *Augustina Regina*, Rear Admiral James Narsalii of the 1st Fleet, and Vice Admirals Charles Codsworthy and Holana Kanjii took seats around the clear table. Not a smile displayed. Starcastle made no apology, no denial; it had been planning to destroy the Corporates for one hundred and seventy years. This did not make the reality of the struggle less grim.

Likely, few Belters had believed ten years ago that the Titan Colony's desperate plea to Starcastle for military aid against their overlords would be answered. At that time they had no idea how well Corporate foolishness had fit into Augustus Kittmore's long-established plans. Starcastle had been waiting seventy years for that request.

Dropping the cube into a slot on top of her desk, she leaned back and watched the brief note appear in green letters on a screen which slanted up from the desk surface. She read aloud:

ADMIRAL MIA YEASAVICH,

I AM SORRY TO INFORM YOU THAT TALKS WITH CORPORATE AND CITY-STATE LEADERS HAVE BROKEN DOWN. THEIR EXTERMINATION EFFORT AGAINST THE TRIBES OF EXCLUDEDS HAS BEEN RESUMED. AND A NEW FLEET IS UNDER CONSTRUCTION IN EARTH ORBIT. THE MATTER IS NOW IN YOUR HANDS.

ALEXANDER

Mia looked up at the tight faces before her. With a steady hand she reached to a projection of icon symbols and tapped in a coded sequence, received a green light, then touched a final key to define battle plan seven. These codes would produced the first radio transmission sent from the flagship in nearly thirty days.

Everyone in the room turned to a thirty-foot circle displayed on the curved wall. A diagram of the planetary system out to three million miles appeared. It was divided into fifteen wedge-shaped sections, one for each fleet under Mia's command. Now, she would see if they had lost any ships over the long wait. Her gaze, and that of Marsha Frost, was fixed on the 3rd Fleet, where their son was. At the moment Luna orbited through that sector.

A twinkle of light appeared.

On her screen the name *Terra Curl* appeared, a cruiser in the 1st Fleet. Other sparkles of light announced three battleships of the 2nd Fleet: *Domus Astra, Mira IV,* and *Promising Sky.* The transport microworld *Cybel* in the 14th Fleet acknowledged its presence. As the speed of light allowed, the more distant elements of the armada began to twinkle on the wall screen.

At last the name of the starship *Titan III* glowed up at her;

she and Marsha exchanged tiny smiles. Their son's ship was still in one piece.

Now the wall of her office began to sparkle with dozens of simultaneous acknowledgments. It looked like a fireworks show. That, she thought, comes next. In all, 367 ships of the line and over a thousand transport vessels began executing the Admiral's battle orders.

"Now, my friends," Mia began, then paused a second, "we will invade the mother planet. Let us hope we may do so gently." But she knew that if the Corporates and other city-states stood by Glades, a slaughter of unbelievable proportions would ensue and forever haunt her soul.

15

Sam turned onto his left side and received a spike of pain; he tried his right with the same result and at last gave up on comfort. He sat up in bed and looked out the balcony window at palms that glowed blue from floodlighting. The discomfort in his abdomen had two ugly heads: a stabbing every time he moved and twisted a gut, and a dull background ache to remind him that he was dying. Silk sheets didn't register much through those two.

A light, salty breeze hinted at perfect weather outside. Yet two touring ships had changed course away from Key West yesterday like the town sat in the eye of some hurricane. Perhaps it did.

Sometime tomorrow, he realized, the Assembly would vote on what Kenton White had been pushing for months—Sam Phoe's removal from office. Word of his ill health had spread despite promises of silence from everyone who knew. Likely the town fathers would call it "retirement." Whatever passion this might have stirred in him paled with each new burst of pain. Remaining mayor was a moot issue. Regardless of Doc's efforts, he would not live much longer. He thought of Tom's quiet funeral, and wondered if he should leave instructions for his own.

His mind squirmed away from this idea to other thoughts.

Soon, he must persuade the Fundy elders to take their people and leave Key West. Well—

A splitting agony tore from his crotch all the way to his throat.

"Whale piss! Death, have you no patience?" he shouted between clenched teeth.

As if showing contrition, the pain abated.

Returning to thoughts of the night before, Sam remembered the hulking man he had made love to. Pip was unbelievably sensual. A stallion in heat he was, but the man never allowed that to prevent mutual pleasure. Sam wished he had stayed. His parting note, cryptic as it was, left Sam wondering.

Why Pip left, Sam understood. Risk. But what did the boy mean by ". . . remember, Auggy Kittmore never took 'no' for an answer to anything"?

Sam hadn't mentioned Auggy to Pip. How then did he know Sam had ever met the man? Between spasming and needle thrusts, he reflected on what things he had refused Auggy. He hadn't joined him to work on his special project—likely that was Starcastle. He had also refused to have children with Auggy. Even rumors of exogenetics drove the Corporate Council to a paranoid frenzy. And between gays! Whatever Pip meant would have to wait until he saw him again, which was likely never.

Someone drove a railroad spike into his back.

"That does it!"

An acrid flavor of metallic copper coated Sam's tongue as he opened his brain link. He reversed its body monitor to induce electrical flow into his nerves. Overexcited, the pain cells stopped firing. Now, he could breath without torture.

Sam drifted into a hazy aqua glow. An underwater cave. The shaft grew darker and darker as he moved into it. Bottom was sable nothingness.

With a start he woke. Sweat covered him. As he sat up in bed the lighting automatically rose to a green luminesce. But he was no longer alone in the room.

"If you've come to murder me, bless you," Sam said, as he swung from the bed and stood.

The skinny figure wearing only overly large black trunks stepped into the light. "Lord Sam, I. . . ." Gibb went to his knees and began crying. His low sobs filled the bedroom.

"You look worse than on the morning I picked you off that beach!" Despite a renewed spiderwebbing of pain across his stomach, Sam knelt down and hugged the boy. He smelled like a ripe sewage pond. Nevertheless, Sam kissed Gibb's forehead, then leaned the boy's head onto his chest. The trembling in his own body confirmed what he had begun to suspect. "You want to hear something insane from a man old enough to be your great grandfather's father? Well, I'll say it anyway. Gibb, I'm in love with you."

The youth stopped sobbing and turned giant black eyes on him. He said nothing, but grabbed Sam more tightly and again buried his head warmly against Sam's chest.

"Come on. We got to clean you up before one of the robots puts you out with the garbage."

Sam led Gibb into the bath and shoved him inside the sonic shower, then joined him. The boy appeared to come back to life as clouds of orange-scented water vibrated about him. Sam took intense delight in watching his tawny body—with a boy's smoothness yet with a man's perfection of musculature. Key West's food had filled him out some. His curly black hair refused to lie flat even when sopping wet and stuck out at odd angles, making him look like a son of Medusa. For him, Sam would gladly turn to stone; in fact, part of him already had.

"The Fundies are after me."

Sam shook his head. Too intoxicated by Gibb's beauty and soothed by the humid touch of the shower vapor, he said only, "Tell me about that tomorrow."

When Gibb finished, they crawled into bed. A faint grayness outside told of nearing dawn. Pushing down or ignoring his pain, Sam Phoe made love to the youth he had so often dreamed of. Reality outshone fantasy.

But with ejaculation came an orgasm of pain for Sam. He groaned and twisted into a ball. Only with intense concentration did he again activate his brain link and squelch the torment with an electrical surge. He could have left this current on and avoided recurring bouts of torture, but such would have left his mind in a misty half-reality, unable to separate dream from fact. That he reserved for the last moments of his life.

Gibb sat up in bed, looking on in horror. "Lord Sam, what's wrong?"

He rubbed the young man's smooth leg. "I'm dying. After two hundred and seventeen years of putting up with my bad habits, my body's quitting!"

"Somebody must help!" The look of consuming anguish on Gibb's face told Sam that he had a new lover, no matter how briefly.

"Doc Pulski's working on it. Though I feel like a child's wall of sand on some beach. Each wave undermines me and washes me lower. This one doesn't topple me, but surely the next will." Seeing the shock on Gibb's face, Sam pulled the boy down close to him and changed subjects: "Tell me how you got in here."

Sam listened for the time between a gray dawn and rosy morning as Gibb recounted who his father was—he wasn't bedding a waif after all!—his run-in with Brio, and a dangerous passage along the seawall. Sam smiled at the behavior of his cybermissiles. Perhaps Narlo programmed them, he thought. More likely it was *Bitch*'s doing. Gibb said nothing more about his conflict with the Fundies, Sam noticed, and mentally increased the size of problem this might be.

"I think I should have been more honest with Brio. The boy's hopes expanded from my silence," Sam said.

He watched a frown cross Gibb's face, but the youth

didn't share whatever thought troubled him.

At some point they both drifted into a brief nap, awakening with the arrival of Sam's usual oatmeal and black tea. The palace computer system always knew when he had a guest and so sent along a vast sampling of breakfast dishes. After a second quick clean-up, they ate on a table in the morning room. It was nine A.M. and the ocean sparkled up at them. A mild February breeze teased their skin.

For an hour Sam told his new lover stories that forced the boy to gobble bites of egg between bouts of hysteric laughter. But at last he stopped. Sam watched Gibb's face become sober.

"I made love to a Fundy."

When Sam got his mouth closed, he said, "For God's sake why, Gibb? With your looks there aren't three gay people on this island who'd refuse to bed you. And those three are comatose! Why a Fundy?"

Gibb began to relate his story. In the middle Sam yelled, "A girl!" and buried his head in his hands. When the youth finished, he sat looking at Sam with his wide eyes. But all the mayor could think was "why me?"

"You have fucked one of their prophets."

"Huh?"

Sam explained that the Fundy sect always proclaimed two seers to interpret the will of God, one aged and one young. Dawn, as Gibb called her, was Debra Fordac, the Prophet of Dawn, and daughter of the Fundy Captain. A fact that Sam had discovered only the day before.

He scratched at the scar on his chin. "Gibb, if you had looked for a way to sabotage my relationship with the Fundies, you couldn't have chosen better! Are you sure you don't work for Sudger?"

"I asked God for one night in your arms. He gave it. Now, they can have me."

Sam Phoe reached a hand forward and placed it behind Gibb's head, pulling him into a kiss. "Over the crushed remains of a dozen cybermissiles and my mangled body! At my age I don't let go of young lovers easily."

Gibb's eyes widened. "No, Sam. Don't destroy the city for my sake!"

"You're getting as bossy as Kenton White, and a lot sooner!"

Sam watched him turn the color of sunrise and lower his gaze to the tabletop. Rubbing the young man's tightly curled black hair, and feeling his trembling, he said, "Let me play this one by ear, okay?" The boy nodded, not looking up.

A bell rang.

"Enter." Sam watched Brio Dirrenni walk down from the living room, onto the terrace, and into the morning room. His eyes were red and black-circled, his skin appeared slacker than usual, and he wore his clothing tightly closed—odd for a youth who always liked to display a perfect body. A white scarf wrapped even his neck.

With a rasping voice he said, "Captain Fordac wishes to see you, Mayor."

Sam noticed that he scrupulously avoided looking at Gibb. But when Sam asked Brio to let the Fundy Captain up, the youth didn't move.

"Yes, Brio?"

The anguish of someone damned played across his face. Brio's eyes never left Sam's, but tears streamed down his face. "I'm responsible for killing those people in the stadium. I gave Glades agents the codes so they could get to the missiles."

"I know. The Fundies are very thorough."

Brio's mouth dropped open. "I didn't realize what the agents were going to do."

"The ones that did know are dead." Sam remembered he had refused them a hearing. The Fundies took that as a hint and cut the men's throats. It was not one of Samuel Phoe's shining moments, he realized.

Key West, 2720 A.D.

Now Brio did lower his gaze. "I tried to do the job myself. He"—Brio nodded toward Gibb, at last acknowledging his presence—"stopped me."

"Boy, that was impertinent! I'll tell you when your services are no longer required! Now, go bring Fordac up here before he starts chewing on Narlo's new furniture."

He watched Brio leave. A bit more spring showed in the youth's step. "What did you interfere with?"

"He tried to hang himself."

Sam realized that Gibb had saved him a massive dose of guilt. If Brio had succeeded, Sam would never have forgiven himself for allowing a youth in his charge to stray so far. But what would he do with Brio now? Could he trust the boy? Something inside him answered "yes."

A clanging of boots on tile announced that Fordac and other Fundy officers had entered the living room. Sam rose from the table slowly so as not to renew the cycle of pain. Clicking open his mental link, he told the house, *Arm*. It was unlikely that the Fundies would try and take Gibb from him by force; it was against their tradition to defy him. He would take no chances, however. He said to Gibb, "Come along."

Fordac and two of his lieutenants stood in the living room of Sam's apartment. He could hear one of them grinding his teeth. This isn't going to be easy, Sam thought.

"Hail, Samuel!" all three shouted. They glared at Gibb.

Captain Fordac lowered the wrap from across his bearded face before he spoke. "We have come for that one." He aimed his finger at Gibb. "He has defiled a guardsman by sexual contact. Under our agreement with you and the city, this person called 'Gibb' shall die by our hand. Is this not so, Samuel?"

The men, Sam noticed, smelled of nervous sweat. But what of his contract with the Fundies? Ah ha! "No, Captain. This is *not* so. You have explicit right to defend the young. You have explicit right to protect your people from homosexual advances. Is Dawn a child under sixteen?" Sam watched Fordac begin to redden as the man understood his tack. "Is Dawn a male?"

Fordac unclenched his jaw to speak. "This foul unbeliever has defiled our prophet! My daughter!"

"Was she raped?"

The Captain took several ragged breaths. The other two men shifted their stance for quick action. But Fordac merely raised his arm and pointed at Sam; the man's hand trembled with repressed fury.

"This time, Samuel, God does not punish us. *You* punish us! You betray us! The elders shall decide."

With those words all three men turned and stomped out. Sam Phoe was left with one distinct impression. He had never before in a hundred and eighty years had to waste a second thought about the Fundy Guard's loyalty. Whatever their elders decided, he could never again be certain of his and the city's human defenders.

16

There was no grand ceremony as there should have been, but the following day both Sam and Gibb signed and sent to the town records department Notice of Joining. They were married. Sam's main motive was love. But this act would also demonstrate to the Fundies precisely how determined he was to protect the boy.

Sam enjoyed the breeze flowing across his skin and listened to Gibb and Narlo chatting over bowls of sliced bananas. Their voices and the clink of silverware echoed slightly inside the green marble gazebo. As usual, his older lover did most of the talking.

Narlo twittered on about Sam as if Sam were on the Moon: "My biggest problem with Sammy is he's sooo tight with money. If I had to run this house on what he wants to give me—Oh! we'd eat grits off tin plates! Half the house would be closed—imagine! And there wouldn't be a cut flower in the place!"

Gibb merely nodded. The boy looked hypnotized by Narlo's white-gloved fingers as they danced before him, providing emphases for the man's onrunning gossip.

As the wind abated slightly, an odor of newly cut grass wafted in about them.

"He's also a brute." Narlo did eye Sam this time, making

doubly sure he was out of striking range. "You do the least thing to provoke him, and he'll abuse you."

Sam tossed in: "Gibb can take care of himself. He once tried to cut my throat."

Gibb turned scarlet and stared at his empty bowl.

Narlo looked at the boy, shook his head. "It *sounds* like you two will make a matched set." He delicately removed the glove from his left hand, reached it over to Gibb's forearm, and squeezed. "Muscles!"

With this Gibb looked up, but closed his eyes. Tears flowed out and glistened down his cheeks.

"What did I say?" asked Narlo, alarm showing on his face.

But the boy shook himself out of some private grief and, reaching across to him, hugged and kissed Narlo. The man in turn used a clean linen napkin to dry Gibb's face.

"There, there."

Those two, Sam realized then, would get along just fine. There had been doubt in his mind; he still remembered the screaming bouts between Narlo and Kenton—loud enough to shatter crystal! Sam used to hide in the command center atop the palace roof to escape the noise. Now he knew why men with less than two-hundred-room houses had only one mate.

Yesterday had been a good day, laced with hope. Besides finally admitting to himself that the tortoise of love had clamped its jaws onto his balls, he had gotten two pieces of prime news. Kenton White had lost his bid to oust The Mayor Forever. By now most of the city knew that Sam Phoe was dying, and this had worked against White. The Assembly had refused to dishonor Sam in what might be his last days.

He must have been grinning widely, for Narlo asked: "What canary did you swallow, Sammy?"

"I was thinking about Kenton White."

"Stop that! Things thought about happen!" said Narlo, waving his hands in any and all signs against evil omens he could think of.

The second item of good news had arrived from Doc

Pulski. It seemed that sometime after leaving Key West Pip had transmitted medical research files to the clinic. Doc had been amazed. "Worth their weight in gold!" he had cried over the holo. Doc could not understand how such information had been left out of the medical data base. Sam knew. It came from Starcastle. Still, all wasn't that rosy. The drug that might help Sam's condition—a chemical flagged by Pip—was a molecule related to Lifestend, but so complex that Key West's synthesizers couldn't reproduce it. Doc refused to give up and was tying together four divers pieces of equipment, trying to produce the medication Sam needed.

A sharp and radiating back pain reminded him that the good doctor had better hurry.

Distant popping noises caught Sam's attention until the pounding of waves below the gazebo again covered it over.

The robot, Private, emerged from the arches of the Grand Salon and crossed the finely clipped grass to them. It halted before him. "Mayor, the Fundy Guard has not taken its positions this morning."

Sam had feared they might abduct Gibb or try some other violent action; he had never considered that they might go on strike. "Well, no one's going to storm the palace. If we need, later, we'll put the cybermissiles out again."

"Yes, Mayor. But the Fundies have locked themselves in their barracks. They have not taken any post in the city this morning. We are without police."

A groan arose from Gibb. "Its all my fault!"

"What did he do?" asked Narlo.

"I made love to a Fundy."

"Oh, God," Narlo whispered. "Sam, will the people turn on us? I know I've spent—God knows, I've spent!—but it wasn't their money was it? I mean. . . ."

"Shhhhh, Narlo. It'll be all right." Sam screeched his chair back and rose, patting the top of Narlo's head. He wasn't sure whether he was lying or not.

A loud thump rolled up to them from lower on the hill,

vibrating and shaking the crystal on the table. Tinkling gravel announced Brio as he came running around the east end of the palace.

"Mayor, somebody's blasted open the main gate! There aren't any Fundies anywhere!" Brio panted out.

"Oh, Sammy! I couldn't face a guillotine! I just couldn't—I would look sooo terrible in sack cloth! Not once did I say anything about eating cake...."

Sam, Gibb, and Brio left a fretting Narlo behind as they raced around the grass-covered terrace platform to the front of the palace. Across the pond toward the main entry, flashing between rows of palms, they could see six or so carts filled with men plus several dozen more on foot charging up the graveled driveway. They were armed.

"Shall I release the cybermissiles, sir?" asked Brio.

"No. Let's go see who has called on us so rudely."

They continued around the corner of the massive stone building, walking to and then down the main stairway to ground level. The first car of gray-uniformed men pulled up before them. Someone in Key West had set up a private army right under his nose, Sam realized. The someone arrived in the second cart.

Kenton White, a laser pistol hanging from his belt, as handsome as ever, stepped out and stood before Sam. A grin crossed his face. He eyed Gibb up and down for a second, then returned his attention to the mayor.

Folding his arms behind him, Sam said: "Is this a coup, Kenton?"

The grin turned to scowl. He pointed toward the men at his back, some carried compact missile launchers, others laser carbines. "These men are the Home Guard. I formed them when I realized that our city was defended by people who hated our life-style and who we are!"

"A coup, Kenton?" Sam repeated, with an edge to his voice. His ear tips were burning.

Kenton White again faced the mayor. He drew in a deep breath. "No, Sam. This is not a coup! Your damned palace computers—with no Fundies around to operate them—wouldn't allow us or a message through the gate. Sam, Sugarloaf and Cudjoe are under attack! Key West is this minute being surrounded by Glades floaters and warships!"

The Fundies, Sam realized, reflecting on his poor judgment, were the only people he had trained to operate the town's defense system.

17

Gibb knew exactly what he must do. So, when the commotion around Lord Sam and Kenton White boiled into a froth, Gibb trotted away unnoticed down the gravel road toward the main gate. The city might be destroyed without its army. He must surrender himself to the Fundies.

The afternoon sun was hot and the wind still. Insects chewed at the hibiscus bushes while darting lizards chewed at the insects.

More of the Home Guard poured in through the open gates to Whitehead Palace. None took note of Gibb. He knew the way out of Sam's complex of buildings only because he had seen the entire place from above, atop the Assembly Building, two nights before. The walls of the Fundy Barracks lay directly ahead across Conch Plaza, but its entry gates were below on Truman Avenue. Groups of men and women hurried up from the lower plaza to the upper one and into the government house. Their pace bespoke urgency.

Distant sounds of raised voices from the lower city bounced around the enclosing stone walls. The least hint of wood smoke hung in the still air.

Gibb quickly ran down the steps into Lambda Plaza. Directly beyond it lay a park filled with pines that he wished he had known about before. Its resinous odor reminded him of

Key West, 2720 A.D.

the high forests that had provided him a home for five years. But he turned right, out of the plaza and onto Truman, stopping when he reached a deeply overhung inset of the blank Barracks walls.

The vast, shadowy cave echoed his every step. He slowed his pace as he advanced on a single reflective steel door as tall as four men and half as wide. His heart pounded. For the first time Gibb felt a chill from his sweat-dampened shirt. He forced the thought of dying from his mind.

How would he get inside?

But as he reached the gate, it was slowly and silently swallowed by the white wall. Cold air puffed out at him, sending a shiver down his back. He faced a wide hallway, dimly lighted at its far end. The corridor's whiteness reinforced light reflecting off what appeared to be distant vegetation in a garden courtyard; it gave the passage a greenish glow. Gibb stepped inside, and the steel gate slid back into place. An echo mocked each step he took. It seemed to say: *stupid boy, stupid boy.*

Where were the Fundies?

A scraping click reverberated down the hall. Gibb froze. He recognized the sound. Someone threw off the safety on a projectile weapon.

Just ahead Gibb could see the shadowed depressions of what appeared to be doorways. It was hard to tell because of the glare from the far end of the hall. In one of these a person moved. Raising his hands high over his head, Gibb remained still. The figure, black against the bright light, slowly advanced.

"Why do you desecrate our home?" The voice was young, high, and reedy.

Gulping down a lump in his throat, Gibb replied, "I did not intend that. My name is Gibb; I came to give myself up to your Elders. I am the one to blame for your people not being at their posts. Key West's being attacked!"

"You are the one who has dishonored the Prophet. You must die."

Gibb felt sweat creeping down his back. His raised arms felt like lead weights. "That's why I came. I don't want the city destroyed for my sake."

"How noble." A tone of sarcasm made the words sharp. "But you are a bit late. Move down the hall!"

Hands still in the air and the ache now spread into his shoulders, Gibb walked toward the green square of light. His eyes began to tear from its brightness. The hall opened at an angle onto a portico. This covered walkway surrounded an orchard of various fruit trees. Below these, red-and-green-speckled, berry-producing bushes hugged the trunks. Black gravel paths ran between trees.

"Take the center path," said his guard, from behind him.

On the far side of the two-hundred-foot-wide courtyard a set of oak doors with twin crosses carved into them confronted him. He halted, but when the guard approached, they swung open into a high-ceilinged room filled with an opaline view of the ocean beyond. It was a projection, for the Barracks had no windows to the outside. In one corner, back to Gibb, a lone figure sat on a stool; to the other side a collection of young men and women stood in a cluster. They were dressed in Fundy white, but their handsome faces were uncovered.

"He has come, Holy One," said Gibb's armed escort.

Slowly, Gibb lowered his aching arms.

The figure turned from the "window" and faced him with her beautiful green eyes. Before now, he had never seen her silky blond hair. "They are dead, Gibb. Of my people, only the dozen of our own Excludeds that you see before you remain alive. The Elders took great offense at Samuel's cavalier actions. I tried to dissuade them—but they left the island very early this morning."

Gibb felt blood flow from his head. Would he die for nothing? "I'm here. I've given myself up! Can't you call them back?"

"From the grave, Gibb?" Her tone sounded distant.

"They departed directly into the Glades fleet. My Father is dead as are the rest. None has survived."

"But, Dawn, how can you be sure?"

She rose from her stool, walked to Gibb, and, reaching up a hand, rubbed a finger along his cheek. "I was sure before we made love that night."

Gibb trembled. He didn't know why. At least it no longer appeared likely that they would kill him.

Dawn turned to the small group that she had named "Excludeds," though he couldn't see why at first glance. Perhaps they had simply disagreed. She said, "You must understand. This young man, Gibb, is my husband—"

Open-mouthed shock distorted the faces of the Fundies. Gibb suspected the same expression covered his. One of the group cut off her words.

"But, Holy One, he is a sodomite. Now Samuel's boy besides!"

"Why do you speak ill of your brother?" she said, and Gibb realized that there was such a thing as a gay Fundy. Dawn's eyes snapped at them as anger whipped across her face. "Would you deny my son a father?"

To a person they averted their eyes from her glare.

Gibb's one-time chief, Onalsey, often had spoken of the jelly knees and the sinking fear that overcomes a man confronted by One Who Truly Knows. Gibb felt that draining. It overpowered any joy he might capture from knowing he had helped bring new life into the world. His head spun.

Ignoring her fellow Fundies, Dawn enveloped him in a warm hug, one which halted his chills. Hot tears washed his neck. She whispered in his ear: "You possess both natures. You must live in both worlds."

She released him, then turned and looked at the remnant of her people. They were silent now, their heads bowed. Nodding at them, she said, "We are few, but we must help Samuel defend our city as best we can. The hand of God will smash

Samuel's enemies. But if we fail to help, blood will fill this sea, and our victory will be as hollow as a lost soul!"

Somewhat begrudgingly Sam took Kenton White and three of the man's officers up to the command center. Brio and Private came too. It was a clear-domed structure some thirty feet across located on the palace roof above his suite. Directly out of the elevator, they faced a giant holo stage where the building's computers could create any visual image Sam might wish to conjure. The party turned left. He stopped before a raised platform with twin chairs.

"There's a match to this room three levels below the Fundy Barracks. To link our defenses completely, the second post must be manned," said Sam.

"We can man it!" Kenton White spoke fervently.

"Takes months of training. One error risks the entire operation. Come have a seat." Sam stepped up onto the raised area, took the farther chair, and swung an instrument panel over to him. "You always wanted to feel in control; here's your chance."

White scowled at him, but took the left-handedly offered seat.

Sam turned his head most of the way around the dome: all hazy sky and brown clouds. Nevertheless, the sun shone hotly through the clear dome; he perspired, and hoped it was from the heat. He keyed a code to lower the air temperature slightly. Very little was done automatically in this room. He tried for a satellite connection; however, Glades had already chopped off or jammed all outside comm lines. Another key stroke sent four holo cameras up sixty feet atop metal poles. Sam flipped on a view of Sugarloaf and Cudjoe.

The clear dome directly before them glowed for a second, then transformed to a jumpy tapestry of white and gray smoke sewn together by threads of flame. The entire picture was hazy. Beyond this wispiness was a silvered battle floater—its weapon-bristled, globular surface glinting whenever the smoke parted sufficiently. Glades had slaughtered ten thousand people in a span of minutes.

Clear sky returned to the dome ceiling.

Sam felt pain in his hands. He looked down at clenched white fists. He unballed them. Kenton's visage, Sam noticed, had become wan.

"Do we have a chance, Sam?" the younger man asked. His deep baritone faltered slightly.

"I'll tell you in a minute."

The sunlight outside faded slightly as Sam activated the palace's reflective shielding, wishing as he did so that the entire town had it. He brought up a large, flat screen in the center of the holo stage. A map of Key West and the adjoining islands appeared in black. The enemy encircled them by clustering gunboats at four positions—the cardinal points—around the island. Oblong red blips, six to the cluster, defined ships at sea level. Flashing round circles stood for airborne floaters, an even dozen scattered around the island at random. Thirty-six war craft in all. These could carry upward of five thousand cybermissiles!

A smattering of green dots tracked the slow, underwater migration of the city's mines into alignment with their Glades targets.

Rotating his chair, he faced his ex-lover, looked into the man's deep blue eyes. Physically, Kenton never failed to stir Sam. "We have only one real chance. Hold them off till they change their minds about destroying us."

"And what would do that?"

Sam shrugged. "They're already doing one stupid thing. They've clustered their gunboats. Our cybermines are creeping under them now. If they're dumb enough to stay put, we'll trim them down to size in a hurry. We got laser cannon here at Whitehead. Add to those two dozen cybermissiles. . . . Do you remember how much you bitched in the Assembly when I ordered *Bitch in Heat?*"

White blushed and looked away.

"Well, she has the firepower to stop hordes of cybermissiles, that will make the difference between staying alive and not."

"Sam, what's to stop them from lobbing a bomb over here and flattening us?"

The mayor shook his head. "Won't be a bomb. I'll bet Roscoe Thorsel is behind this. He wants the city—at least its infrastructure. No bomb. He'll toss nerve toxin at us. Then scoop up the bodies. Thousands of cybermissiles and it only takes a couple of good hits."

"That's comforting!"

Sam turned to Private, who stood quietly to his left, sunlight glinting off its porcelain skin, and asked: "Where's Gibb?"

"I do not know, Samuel. Without the Fundies our input is sparse."

First retracting the flat screen, Sam entered a private code for the Glades general. After a minute's wait, the platform glowed and blue sparks flitted in the air above it. The image that appeared was of a plump and balding man. Seated, his bent posture gave the impression of some enthroned dwarf king.

Grinning, Roscoe Thorsel said: "Ah, the chief faggot!"

"Good afternoon to you too, Roscoe. You know I'm going to kill you for what your ships did today," Sam said in an even voice.

The grin vanished. "You all are invited to try, faggot!"

"Roscoe, timing for attacking us wasn't too sharp on your part."

"How's that?" The man rubbed his chin. Ghostlike, blurred images appeared behind him, other officers, all out of focus.

Sam glanced at Kenton's three ranking men who had come up to the command center with them. All were young, not a one had reached thirty, perhaps a year's total training amongst them.

Key West, 2720 A.D.

Sam felt ancient. "It's like this, Roscoe. Sudger thinks the rebels in the Belt are under control, but the truth is they're coming for Earth."

The man's face didn't react. He already knew it.

"Maybe. Sudger said you'd been meeting with 'em. Well, they won't care much who owns this little rock. Tough luck, faggot!" The image flashed off.

Sam listened to low breathing. All eyes were on him. At last Kenton White asked, "Is that true, Sam—about the Belters?"

First stretching broadly, and thus realizing that his legs were numb, Sam replied, "I told that to fat Roscoe hoping it would make him think—thinking always slows him down." Chuckling echoed in the room, "But it's true. As best I can tell, the Corporate Council is losing the biggest and most secret war in human history."

"But, Mayor, sir, no one's seen a shot fired," said a baby-faced young man with short-cut red hair. He wore the silver bars of a captain. For the first time spotting the tiny star on the man's collar, Sam realized Kenton had made himself a general!

"It's all been fought it space. The Corporates have lost everything beyond Luna. And the Belters have cleared their allies among the Excludeds away from all the city-states in preparation for an attack. I have every reason to believe that the world as we know it will not exist in a month's time."

Sam's words had drained color from all the men. Nothing affected Private. He took in fact and fiction, weighed them, then reshuffled his world model accordingly.

Kenton White placed a mildly trembling hand on his shoulder. "We'll be a footnote in some history book. One small island crushed between colossi!"

"Whale piss! Nobody gave you permission to be pessimistic. Private, patch us in to *Bitch*."

The robot spoke softly, but its words demolished Sam. "She is out, sir."

"*Out!*"

"Yes, sir. Alexander of Titan took *Bitch* and Sergeant two days ago. He did not file a destination—"

Sam's ears were on fire. Pip had stolen his ship! "How could he break her security codes?"

"But, sir, why would they need breaking? He has full access—"

Sam cut the robot off. "Shut yourself off and carry out a detailed program audit!"

The machine had a hurt look on its face, but walked to one side of the circular room and stood. Obviously, Pip had been able to cut through Sam's guard programs so thoroughly that the computers didn't even realize they had been violated. Without *Bitch* the people of Key West were walking corpses.

"Kenton, you now have my permission to be pessimistic."

18

The emergency bell tinged.

"There they come!" shouted Brio.

Everyone in the command center watched the curved surface of the dome as a magnified projection of six sleek, gray gunboats released cybermissiles. Hundreds of them caught the light while twirling upward. Then they circled the boats. And this was only one of four fleets performing the same deadly act.

But Sam's gaze fastened to the tactical picture on a smaller screen beside his chair. He couldn't tell from the diagram before him precisely how close the city's mines had been able to creep.

"Whale piss!"

He tapped a key that would send his cybermissiles and *Whelp I* into the air. The Glades missiles were incompetents compared to his, but sheer numbers mattered. Key West was about to become a second Alamo.

Sam jumped slightly when his tactical screen flashed. It settled back to a crisp view with ten times the detail it had given only moments before. Someone had activated the second command post! The mines needed another five minutes to site in under those gunboats and their clouds of cybermissiles.

A familiar, boyish face, topped by curly hair, flashed onto a small "window" of the tactical monitor. "Hi, Sam!"

"Gibb, where the hell are you?"

A wide grin filled his face. "At the Fundy Barracks. All but thirteen of them left early this morning. Dawn says they were killed by Glades warships." Sam felt a surge of grief flow over him. "The ones still here say they can operate the control room."

"They're already doing it, and damn good! Listen, you stay underground with them. That room's sealed against nerve toxin."

Sam watched the boy's thickish lips twist down into a pout. "I want to be with you, Lord Sam."

"Stay put!" Sam clicked the window off his screen. One more look into those eyes and he would have relented. Right now Sam Phoe would have sold back a hundred years of his life to place an arm about Gibb's thin waist. *I'm getting both old and maudlin!* he thought.

"Sir, gunboats are beginning to spread!" called the red-headed captain.

"Detonate the mines, Sam!" Kenton White yelled in his ear. "We'll lose our chance at the gunboats."

He could smell the man's nervous sweat. It was a sour odor. The main trouble with Kenton, Sam realized, was that the young man had never learned the art of patience. His mother spoiled him—an endemic problem in the Middle House. He reached a hand over and patted Kenton's shoulder. His shirt felt damp.

Sam concentrated on the pattern of squiggles and circles dancing about the screen. The enemy cybermissiles were a pink haze—really tiny red dots—shifting about a slowly expanding area of red points, which represented the gunboats. A cluster of green specks worked its way into this seething, producing to his eye a blue tinge. He waited.

"Sam, for God's sake! Fire them while they still have a use!" yelled Kenton, as the other officers and Brio edged closer to look over his shoulder.

"Patience, Kenton. Patience."

He watched the red areas spread past the green mines for several more minutes. Then an orange line encircled both and flashed at him: the computers had spotted optimum effect. He hit the key.

Glaring light flashed into the room. Seconds later a low rumble from several directions at once rolled about them. It vibrated his seat.

"Enemy count?" Sam asked the computer.

"WAIT PLEASE, INTERFERENCE," it replied.

Sam glanced at the young men about him. They held their breaths. All but Brio were whiter than they had been before the battle began. It was one thing to put on a uniform, quite another to look down a gun barrel—especially someone else's gun barrel! Brio, however, appeared expectant, as if he thought the Angel of Death might smile at him when no one else would.

REDUCTION OF ENEMY FORCES: ELEVEN GUNBOATS DESTROYED, THREE GUNBOATS DEAD IN THE WATER, AND TWO DAMAGED. TWO FLOATERS DESTROYED. CYBERMISSILES REDUCED BY EIGHTY-SEVEN PERCENT.

A whooping cheer from the young men left Sam's ears ringing.

He clicked a few keys to instruct *Whelp I* and their own cybermissiles to sweep up the remaining enemy missiles. He glanced over at the screen; there were seventy of them left. Likely they were disoriented; this would make them easy targets.

"That showed 'em!" a flushed Kenton White shouted in Sam's ear.

"Maybe. But if we make Roscoe decide the price of having Key West in one piece is too high. . . ." Sam didn't have to complete the thought, for Kenton blanched again.

Something whistled by overhead.

"Shit!" yelled the redhead.

A crashing thump resounded from somewhere in the city.

"It didn't explode!" yelled Brio.

Their cybermissiles had missed one of the enemy's. But if it crashed, likely the thing was totally dysfunctional; these were not mere bombs hurled at distant targets.

A second grinding crunch drowned out all other sounds. The chair beneath Sam tossed forward. Only a strong grip kept him from being thrown atop the computer screens. One hand bled.

Kenton White had not been so lucky. He looked up at Sam from the dais floor, patting a forehead covered by blood. Trying to rise and help the man, Sam discovered what he had suspected earlier: His legs didn't work. He too hit the floor.

"What happened?" White choked out.

"Our missiles blinded a couple of Glades's, and they rammed into the island. That last one hit us at full speed and within a few feet of the palace."

"It didn't hit the building?"

"Alive, aren't you? You're not that injured—help me up!"

As Kenton White assisted him to rise, one of the Home Guard emerged from the elevator panting and trying to rasp a message out to his captain. White called across the room: "What is it?"

The captain listened to the soldier for a second more, asked a question, then said to "General" White, "A cybermissile dug up forty feet of Duval Street in front of the Da Vinci and another rammed into the palace seawall. Neither exploded."

"Anyone hurt?" asked Sam.

The soldier shook his head. "Most everyone's two levels down, Mayor."

"Small price for the damage we did to Glades's fleet!" shouted Kenton.

Sam whispered to him: "But now we've shot our wad. They have thousands of cybermissiles left—we have a couple of dozen."

"Sam, you're depressing!"

"I'm a realist." Holding on to the computer console, Sam leaned away from his ex-lover.

"Are you saying we have to surrender?"

Sam yelled over to the messenger: "Anyone hooked in to either missile yet?"

"Yes, sir. Our men were attaching sensors to the one over on Duval when I left."

With one finger Sam typed in strings of codes until he found the flow of analytical data from the enemy cybermissile. Satisfied, he nodded for Kenton to look at the second screen that stood beside his chair.

The man visibly trembled.

The missile on Duval Street carried over ninety gallons of degradable neurotoxin; in a few hours its poison would be harmless. But meanwhile its content was more than enough to kill a million people. Luckily, it wasn't leaking despite the crash.

"My guess, Kenton, is that Roscoe Thorsel, being an impatient man, threw all his toxic missiles at us in the first round. He's lost them! We may get burned alive or shot full of tiny holes—but the son of a bitch can no longer gas us like cockroaches!"

Gibb was anxious to return to Sam, but he took a minute to circle oceanward of the palace and see where the cybermissile had hit. A mild breeze blew away some of the haze. It was not quite dusk, though the palace's mirror shield cut out some of the last rays, making the entire rear terrace dim. The marble gazebo was a pile of green rocks. Sections of seawall balustrade lay against the archways into the Grand Salon. As he walked farther out on the overlook, Gibb could see that the missile had plowed into Whitehead about three feet below the terrace. Like a mole, it had dug up a ridge.

Someone or something was digging down into the ridge,

tossing out shovelfuls of gray sand tinged with black soil onto the undamaged grass. He looked into the hole.

"Brio! What are you doing?"

The youth scowled at him. "None of your damned business!"

"Will that thing explode?"

"Easy way to be rid of a traitor, huh?"

As far as Gibb was concerned, Brio could stick out his own neck all he wanted, and indulge in self-pity for a thousand years; but now he risked other lives. "If that thing explodes, you won't be the only one to go up. Stop it!"

Brio's shovel clanged against metal. He stopped digging, leaned against the handle, and began an angry retort. Then he stopped and shook his head. "I looked at the fins—hanging out over the ocean. This thing's right side up. If I'm careful, I can reach its decoder box. Know what that is?"

Gibb shook his head and swatted at a gnat.

"It's what tells the missile it's receiving a legitimate command signal. If I get it and we can break the code in time, then we'll control their missiles." With this thought, a wide grin filled his dirt-streaked face.

"I can help you dig, at least," said Gibb.

"No!—thanks. Dirt's off the thing now. A tech's on the way up. Just wish me luck."

Gibb nodded. "That and a prayer."

He left Brio to his project, more at ease knowing it was worth the gamble. Within ten minutes, Gibb reached the palace roof and entered the command center. An annoyed Kenton White pointed him toward the northeast corner of the palace roof, where Gibb found Lord Sam sniffing the evening air and surveying his city. The shiny robot, Private, stood near at hand.

A loud clang arose from Brio's dig. Gibb clamped his eyes closed and waited for the boom.

"Thought I told you to stay put!"

Opening his eyes, Gibb looked into Sam Phoe's white-haired and angry visage. He returned a grin and watched the man's arctic expression melt.

Turning to the side so his vision again took in Whitehead Park and the town below, Sam said, "We've won a battle. Roscoe Thorsel's in charge out there. I know him. Bulldog! We've forced him to stop and think; we haven't stopped him."

"Will we be okay?"

Sam didn't reply. He reached an arm about Gibb's waist and pulled him close. Its warmth sent a rush of desire through Gibb. He wanted to make love to this man, here and now. But Sam didn't look well—his skin had a yellow pallor and he trembled slightly.

"Has the doctor finished your medicine yet?" Gibb asked.

Grinning weakly, Sam reached into his jacket pocket and brought out a thin vial. He set it on a table beside his chair. "Just swallow this, but I'm waiting to take it—"

"Why?" Worry cracked Gibb's voice as he asked.

"Doc said it might or mightn't work and in either case it would knock me out for days. Damn it, Gibb! I'm the only competent military officer in Key West. If I conk out, so does my city!"

"Lord Sam, you look terrible!"

He pointed a finger at Gibb's brown and black stained blue tunic. "So do you! They haven't bombed the laundry yet. Find a clean tunic."

Embarrassed, Gibb looked at the ground. He changed the subject. "It seems I have a wife."

"Whale piss! Not faithful to me for a day even!"

He jerked his head up. But the silver glow cast by the moon sparkled from Sam's amused eyes. "It's Dawn," Gibb added.

"Well, the Fundies were never fond of mothers without

husbands. Sometimes they one-sidedly declare the fact. Don't look for too much intimacy. Was it all animal hormones, or do you like the girl?"

"I love her too, I think."

Kneeling down beside Sam and hugging his nearest leg, which was too cold, Gibb told of his entire relationship with the young Fundy prophet, from Brio's trickery to lovemaking borne of mutual despair. By the end Sam was laughing so hard his eyes teared; he apologized between fits of guffawing.

"Oh, you have had one hard time here! I wasn't laughing at you. You handle yourself damn well. When I was eighteen, I know I didn't have your guts! I'm laughing at a state of affairs that could bring such events to pass. Truly a black comedy!" Sam turned his attention to the robot. "Private, do you think you could bring me a pot of tea without allowing someone to steal it!"

"Yes, Mayor." The robot trotted off toward the command center. Gibb knew that it went physically because Key West tried to eliminate all unnecessary radio and cable transmissions. Every bit of computer power was needed for defense.

The city below them, beyond the high park, shone its browns, blues, and oranges only by moonlight. There were no electric lights. Still, Duval Street churned with yellow flickers and blue shadows down its entire length. A procession of some sort moved along it. The light wind brought wisps of a hymn up to the palace roof.

"Sam, what's going on down there?"

"They're going to the Church of the Secret Lover. Not very logical; cybermissiles could come over any time."

"Their hearts call them," said Gibb, thinking of what Dawn had said about its inner chapel: God was there.

"I'd be among them too, but my legs aren't working to well."

"Sam, you must take the medicine!"

He ignored Gibb's entreaty. His gaze stayed on the slow-moving crowd below. "I have mothered them too much over the years. Now what can I do for them? They trust me to save them! Somehow. But what can I do? What can I give, now?"

"Onalsey talked often of the Old One of the Islands." Sam snorted at Gibb's words, but the boy hugged him all the tighter and continued: "He spoke of a man I never dreamed to be real, much less one that I would share love with. My chief spoke of your fight with the great cities, of your efforts to save the Excludeds. He whispered your name to me when times were hardest. My Lord Sam you will give what you have always given: Hope."

Thudding footfalls cut off the beginning of Sam's retort.

Brio's face and wide, beaming smile glowed in the weak light as he halted before Sam's chair. He held up a metal object that looked like an elongated chicken egg, twice that size and with dangling wires.

"Decoder box from the missile out back!" Brio shouted.

Sam said, "Brio, whatever you've done in the past is forgiven, lad!" He took the device from the young man. "This and a little work gives us a chance!"

A servo cart carrying Sam's tea whined and clattered its way across the roof toward them.

Gibb glanced at it, then down at the table beside a distracted Sam Phoe. He moved away from the animated discussion between the two men who might have become lovers eventually if Sam hadn't pulled Gibb from a Georgia beach. He stopped the cart short of them and fixed the mayor his cup of tea.

Returning, Gibb presented a double-handled mug.

"Oh. Thanks, Gibb." After taking a deep swallow, Sam returned to examine the "egg." A moment later he paused, licked his lips, made a face, and stared up at Gibb. "You bastard!"

As Sam slumped forward, Brio yelled, "What'd you do to him?"

"He wouldn't take his medicine. I gave it to him."

As Brio advanced on him, Gibb shifted his weight, preparing to fight the larger youth.

For a few seconds two moons lighted the night sky. Twin shadows appeard everywhere. To the southeast a vast glowing circle finished expanding, then receded into blackness. Before it died out completely, Gibb saw two of the distant, balloonlike enemy floaters sparkling against indigo water.

"That's the position of a laser platform," Brio said, pointing skyward. His mouth hung open. Then he pointed over Gibb's shoulder.

Warily, keeping an eye on Brio, Gibb turned about and looked north. Silently flashing and pulsing, red and silver light traced the entire northeastern sky. Never had he beheld a thunderstorm with such power.

19

"I don't want anyone ever to think that I didn't love this man. Despite the differences we had, never did I stop loving him." In the room's weak illumination Kenton White's hair, Gibb observed, had taken on the color of silver moonlight. The man noticed Gibb's gaze and glanced away.

"What audience is he playing to?" whispered Narlo.

But Gibb wondered why White talked as though Lord Sam were already dead? The mayor appeared translucently pale in the dim lighting, and his entire body had slowed its living, but he was very much alive.

In the hour since they brought Sam below to his own bed, a near gale had arisen out of the north and howled about the windows. For air, Gibb had left open the west window. Wind worried its pleated drapery, creating a constant flapping sound.

"I must return to the command center." White spoke to no one in particular. "That cybermissile jarred lose the comm lines inside the palace. So, if there's a change, send somebody up for me."

Once Kenton White departed, Narlo leaned over the bed and reached out a hand. The lavender lace cuff on his jacket made an explosive contrast to Sam's wan complexion. (Earlier, at Gibb's staring, Narlo had commented: "I'm dressed to meet my end!") He expelled a jerky sob. "Why is he so cold? Are you sure he's alive?"

"He said thé drug would knock him out," Gibb replied, beginning to feel uneasy about giving his lover Pip's medicine against his will. "Put an ear to his chest."

Narlo removed a wide-brim white hat and leaned his head on Sam. "His heart's beating. But sooo slow . . . thump . . . thump. . . ."

Sounds from the ocean grew ever louder, becoming hammer blows against the seawall. Even from the west window, salt spray splattered onto the tile floor, making it slippery in spots. Maybe the storm delayed the attack against them, Gibb hoped.

Brio entered through the morning room, carrying a tray of food. The automatic kitchen in Sam's suite radioed the main data bank to obtain its recipes, and so wasn't used. But Sam's aide managed to find hot tea and tepid beer, sliced beef and turkey, once-crisply-fried-but-now-soggy eggplant, and dark pumpernickel rolls. He set down his collection on a table near the bed, and collapsed in a chair.

"Best I could do. Power's down," Brio commented to the ceiling.

Gibb left the bedside and joined Brio at the table. He hadn't eaten since breakfast, which felt like a thousand years ago. Rolling a thin slice of beef up into a bite, he watched Brio's shadowed features. It was clear on his face: Lord Sam had forgiven him, but he had not forgiven himself. The youth nibbled at a roll while eyeing the room's bronze chandelier.

Narlo joined them. "Where are the napkins? And the silverware?"

With a sigh, Brio lurched forward, rose, and left the bedroom, returning with plates, utensils, and brown napkins. These he set on the table.

Narlo cleared his throat and eyed the youth.

Brio groaned. He moved around to Narlo's side of the table and set out a place before the man. Then he fluffed open a napkin and placed it on his lap. That completed, Brio proceeded to serve a sampling of everything but the beer, which Narlo sniffed at and waved away.

"Under all conditions, standards must be maintained," said Narlo, as he removed his gloves and began carving his slice of beef into tiny pieces. "This dimness is very like candlelight, without the flickering."

Gibb watched with unbelieving fascination.

"I took the decoder down to the Fundies," Brio said, between bites of roll, now watching the whipping palm trees outside the west balcony. "Girl down there's odd. When I asked her if the decoder would help destroy Key West's enemies, she said they were already destroyed. Those floaters out there aren't our bedmates! Weird girl!"

"Yes, very," Gibb replied through a mental fog. All he could see in the grayness was a pair of soft green eyes.

"Brio, were there no cut flowers?" asked Narlo. "Sammy really should have cut flowers, you know."

"I'll look later, sir." The young aide's voice had lost its edge.

After he finished his roll and half a glass of the warm beer, Brio grunted his way up from the table. Despite a beginning lassitude, he trotted out of the bedroom and returned thirty minutes later, his arms filled with white and pink gladiolas. He stood and smiled broadly.

Narlo frowned and tapped his right foot. "Vases, Brio. Vases! Really, the boy is hopeless."

Gibb couldn't help himself; he began laughing, then couldn't stop. They stared at him. He shrugged an apology, but nothing he did could stop his hysteric chortling. His lungs needed air; he couldn't stop long enough to breathe. Gibb felt warm arms go about him, hug him tightly. When at last he stopped laughing, Gibb looked through tears down into Narlo's round face and doglike brown eyes.

"There, there. My lovely boy, those unwelcome people out there," Narlo flicked his bejeweled hand toward the sea, "and this odd storm have put even my nerves on edge."

Brio reached out a hand and squeezed Gibb's shoulder.

Later, when they were giving an inert Sam Phoe a sponge bath, Kenton White came running in, all out of breath. While he bent over, hands on knees, regaining his wind, rattling palms outside carried on his undisclosed excitement.

"Needles . . . floaters released a cloud of needles!" White rasped.

"What are needles?" Gibb asked.

"Huh . . . like cybermissiles, but much smaller: twelve inches by one inch. They're antipersonnel weapons. The floaters released thousands of them!"

White moved to the south window and pulled back its drape. "That gray cloud is—"

Gibb watched the window shatter, sparkles of glass spraying out into the room. With a sickening bass thud, an object hit Kenton White directly in the chest, knocking him to the middle of the room and under the table. Something wet and sticky was flung across Gibb's face and chest.

Narlo shrieked.

Brio, who was closer, darted across to White. "Ugh! Thing took out his whole chest and kept going." He spread an extra bed cover over the body.

Only then did Gibb notice a small hole in the far wall. He watched as Narlo backed against the wall, as if trying to press his way through it to the outside. He clutched a crystal glass so tightly that Gibb thought it might shatter at any moment. Visible in the moonlight and faint glow from the laser shield, Narlo too was covered by speckles of maroon.

A whizzing roar passed over the palace, rattling the unbroken glass windows. Narlo yelled.

Brio ducked down below the table just as the unopened section of the west window burst into a cloud of glass shards. Gibb hit the floor. But Narlo, eyes wide with terror, stood frozen against the wall.

Key West, 2720 A.D.

The device that entered the room shone a light gray. Its elongated shape produced first a swordlike shadow, then a black circle on the wall opposite Gibb as it floated and turned, seeking a target. He was as paralyzed as Narlo—glued to the floor.

Narlo groaned; it turned toward him.

Brio jumped from cover. "Here I am, bastard!"

As the tiny missile spun about, Narlo flung the heavy glass he had been holding at the "needle." His effort did not damage it, rather the glass knocked it slightly off aim precisely as the thing jetted for Brio. It missed. Distant thumping sounds followed by a muffled crack told Gibb that the missile had torn through several rooms before exploding.

Brio nodded to Narlo. "Thanks."

"An exchange of 'thanks,' I think." Narlo moved shakily to the bed and collapsed on the edge, placed a hand on Sam's chest, and patted. "My expert shot comes from practice throwing things at this one."

"Well," said Brio, "at least they're still trying to take the island."

"What do you mean?" asked Gibb, as he stood again.

The youth wiped at his eyes before replying. "As long as they want our old buildings and new factories, they won't blast us out of here. We couldn't stop a fusion missile any better than we stopped those needles. One flash, no more Key West."

Narlo rose and swayed along toward the south window. Its blowing drape lashed at him. Craning his neck, he peered outside. Moonglow lit him from above as he stepped out onto the balcony.

"Narlo!" Gibb whispered harshly. The man risked his life.

"Must have more air. Smell of blood is making us ill."

A flash of white light silhouetted Narlo for a second before throwing him back into the room. A boom rattled everything around them.

"Shit!" Brio rushed forward, grabbed the small man, and dragged him back behind the protection of the stone wall.

Gibb joined Brio on the floor and began examining Narlo. New blood covered the man's white suit, and the force of the blast had ripped off one of his lace cuffs. Gibb's hands trembled as he unbuttoned Narlo's shirt. It was hard to see, but his wounds appeared more abrasions than punctures or cuts. A piece of shrapnel had left a long gash across his forehead.

A ringing hiss filled the bedroom.

Gibb thought his heart would stop beating. Then the flight of needles passed over into the lower city. Who are they killing below? he wondered, as he cradled Narlo's head and held Sam's cool arm.

Brio reached across Narlo and placed a hand on Gibb's shoulder. "The needles are clearing the way for Glades's troops. We may not have much longer. I'm sorry for what I did to you. You didn't deserve it, no matter how badly I wanted to marry Sam."

Thinking of no reply, Gibb merely nodded.

Something began a low whine that ran up the scale and into a dog's ear, as Onalsey used to say. Flashes lighted the building's exterior. Gibb's heart began to tear at his rib cage. Blood rushed from his head.

"Relax. It's our laser cannons firing. Guess they found a tar—"

Brio froze in midsentence. A needle hissed its way through the south window. It floated in place a mere ten feet from them. Somehow it held itself off the ground without using its jets. The missile began to turn its nose toward them.

They scrambled to either side of its aim. But Brio was trapped to the inside, against the wall. It targeted him. As Gibb had seen when Brio faced death before, the youth closed his eyes and waited.

The needle, however, neither fired its jets nor exploded;

Key West, 2720 A.D. 199

rather the thing settled to the floor like a becalmed kite.

Brio let out a whoop. He danced over to and, jumping, smashed both feet down upon the deadly missile. He shouted, "They broke the code! The Fundies turned 'em off! If Glades hasn't cleared all the Home Guard out of their way, they may not send in troops yet. The Fundies bought us time!"

The purchased time ran out at dawn.

Gibb looked over the south balcony railing. Needles littered the terrace below. How many people, he wondered, did those things kill last night? Workmen ran about in the reddish light, picking up the things by the dozen.

"What are they going to do with them?" he asked Brio, who stood beside him, picking at a bandage patch on his left arm.

"Rewire, reprogram. Maybe find a way to shoot them back."

Returning his gaze to sea, Gibb could barely distinguish the mirror shields of three floaters tinted a deep rose by the new sun. Birds happily twittered at him from the trees below; they weren't at war. Brio shifted positions, crunching broken glass and plastic under foot.

Earlier, when the eastern sky had just become gray, members of the Home Guard had removed their general's body. Yet, the comatose Samuel Phoe held their attention; each man stopped and stood silently over him. Their actions had so reminded Gibb of a funeral that he cried until the men left. He was not alone, for most of the soldiers departed with glistening cheeks. Moments after this, a medperson, sent by Doc Pulski, arrived to check on the mayor.

His heart rate was down to ten beats per minute. He felt like ice. Yet he was alive. The medperson could only shrug. Gibb's guilt over giving him the medicine grew with each slowing beat. Could he really be sure of Pip's intent in sending the formula for that drug? Had Gibb killed the man he loved?

The medperson had also patched the rest of them. Narlo was covered by tiny cuts, but he would recover. His white suit with purple lace wouldn't.

Gibb's mind returned to the balcony.

"They've begun the next round," said Brio, pointing toward the distant globes. Tiny flicks of red and silver light danced around the silvered balls. "Those look bigger than the first missiles. Maybe they've decided to bomb us out. Blockbusters. I guess they must have figured by now that they can always rebuild."

"Let's get Sam down to the Fundy's command room!" Gibb shouted, not wanting his lover exposed to another round like the last.

"He's safer here. The mayor said several times how much Roscoe Thorsel loves this house. He'd blow away all the rest of the island before he'd bomb here. Any case, there isn't time."

Gibb reached out a hand and touched the rail, to steady himself, for he was still shaky. It was damp and sticky with salt blown there by last night's high winds. "Well . . . we almost made it. I mean, Lord Sam thought the Belters might take our part since they aided the Excludeds tribes."

Brio expelled a snorting laugh. "If there's a bigger war going on and even if the Belters win, conquerors like to hear their balls rattle! They'd never help pansies! If neither side kills us, the winner will find some way to rid itself of embarrassing faggots. Old history with a new title! Why should it be different?"

What made Brio's words doubly depressing was their ring of truth.

Roscoe Thorsel scooted back in his chair and stared at the twin tactical screens before him. This had to be right. Already, he had lost so much equipment that Sudger would have his hide for a rug. (Of course he had destroyed the Fundies; that was worth points.) But if he also lost the battle, he would have to take his own life or face the unpleasant method his boss might use.

These cybers would level the island one block at a time, beginning with the south seawall area. Much to his regret, the missiles would commence by destroying Whitehead Palace. Ah, what a loss! he thought. Next, robot landing troops would move in, killing everything in sight. He had left open a route to the sea on the west, hoping the islanders would take to the boats and flee. He would let them, at least until they were beyond sight from land.

He leaned back and scratched his stomach. The floater's control area hummed at him.

"Any word from Glades?" he asked a commander in an adjoining chair. He could have keyed the panel before him, but a human voice was nice.

"Channels are still jammed, General."

He never would have believed that Key West had such sophisticated jamming equipment, capable of totally cutting him off from his city-state. Yet they did. And they had used it, for Glades had snapped off the air the evening before when Thorsel was trying to discover what had happened to the orbital laser platform. Communications had halted like some giant hand had squashed the city. That thought produced a shudder. But he had also tried other channels; they, too, were useless static.

Roscoe allowed his gaze to drift to the window. The silver ball of another floater drifted to their right, some two hundred yards away. Beyond that a dim, gray line on the glimmering horizon defined Key West.

"General! The comms are open again, sir. You'd better hear what's on line one!"

He turned his chair slightly to the left and shifted the broadcast onto a small holostage. The image of Omarel Sinca,

President of the Corporate Council stood before him. The man obviously read his speech from notes off camera:

". . . and as of five thirty this A.M. the Corporate Council of Earth and the Outer Planets has officially dissolved. All authority vested in the Council has passed to His Majesty's Minister for Provincial Commerce and his planetary delegates."

No sooner had Roscoe managed to get his mouth closed than Sinca's figure vanished and the well-known, rotund form of Atwater Dorsettor appeared. He was President of Atlanta and current-year Chairman of the World Assembly of City-States. Dark circles lined the man's eyes. He too read a prepared message:

"An hour ago, the member states of the Assembly severally and individually did by unanimous vote unconditionally relinquished all sovereign authority on this planet to His Majesty's Governor-General Designate, the Viscount Nassel—"

Roscoe snapped off the broadcast. From Sudger's withdrawn behavior over the past year, Roscoe had gathered that the war with the Belters wasn't going well. But total defeat! Unconditional surrender! He had to move fast if he wanted to secure Key West as his before the new overlords took a census.

"Commander, send out word to the troop convoy. They will be landing at once!"

"Yes, sir!"

Roscoe leaned back and watched the cybermissiles begin a final circle of the fleet before diving into the distant town. Too bad, Sam Phoe, he thought. I never really disliked you.

"Sir, we have a priority call!"

"Not now!"

The commander persisted: "Sir, it's coming in on the emergency frequency."

Ten to one a new Glades leadership was calling to stop him. No way! "I don't want to talk to Glades, damn it! Not now!"

A tone of panic leaked into the commander's voice. "General, the caller lists as one Commodore Ipner, and signal origin is from orbit."

With a sigh, Roscoe opened the channel. An image of a middle-aged black woman stood before him. Her crisp white uniform bespoke authority. A single gold star shone from a stiff blue collar.

"Who is in charge of your fleet?" she asked, her voice icy.

"General Roscoe Thorsel, ma'am. At your service."

"Sir, I am Commodore Joan Ipner of His Majesty's Ship *Seven Days*. My orders are to halt any belligerent activity taking place within my area of posting. This certainly includes your actions against the island of Key West."

"Ma'am, I am here carrying out a small policing action at the order of Glades' president Sudger and—"

"General Thorsel, Glades City-State no longer exists."

Her words took Roscoe aback. It had never occurred to him that the Belters might go beyond merely controlling deep space. Could he trust what this female officer told him? No!

"I believe I will follow through with the last of my orders, Ma'am."

Roscoe knew that his ships' armor and laser shielding were state of the art. He was safe, and the commodore would likely have to report this problem elsewhere. By then he would have Key West.

His gaze wandered up to the window. The distant other floater closed toward Key West, preparing to launch its cybers. But as he watched, it appeared to jump, almost as if he were watching a poor video display rather than the real scene. A second later the floater vanished in a flash of light and fragments.

Sound buffeted him. Shock waves nearly tossed him from his chair.

Breathing raggedly, fists clenched into balls, Roscoe Thorsel awaited his turn.

But the image, still floating above the holo stage, said: "Do I have your attention, General Thorsel?"

Roscoe whispered huskily, "Yes, Ma'am. You surely do."

20

Two days after the end of fighting, Sam Phoe began to pull out of the coma.

Gibb could see Lord Sam's eyes flicker open. The boy reached a hand over to where Pip sat looking out the window and pulled at his arm. The big man rose and came quickly to the bedside.

Sam's eyes turned toward him; he blinked. "You stole my ship."

"I had to, Sam. It took your sub to get me back to my shuttle. Without the ringmaster, the circus wouldn't have come to town."

The mayor seemed to accept this: he nodded. His gaze wandered to Gibb. A smile lit his face. And it was the face that amazed Gibb, for all the wrinkles and discoloration that had been there mere days before were gone. Pip had already explained to Gibb that Sam's one-time lover and Pip's grandfather, Auggy Kittmore, had given Sam a custom formulation of Lifestend. A second dose was long overdue, so Sam began to age rapidly. Gibb had "poisoned" him with his second dose—just in time.

With a cracking voice, Sam asked, "How many people did we lose?"

"Two hundred and ten, Lord Sam. Kenton White was

killed." As Sam's eyes began to glisten with tears, Gibb added: "He said he never stopped loving you."

Sam nodded, then asked, "Glades?"

"It's gone, Sam," Pip replied. "It was the only city we had to attack."

Samuel Phoe drifted back to sleep as if the destruction of that city meant Key West's defense no longer needed his personal attention. He could rest now.

Gibb bent over and kissed his lover on the forehead.

Outside, construction robots clanked about, repairing damage wrought by the cybermissiles and needles. Faint music from Conch Plaza, where the official surrender ceremony shortly would be held, drifted in through the windows. Gibb's nose ran slightly, allergy activated by the vases and bowls of cut flowers that a still-bedridden Narlo Adamms had ordered sent up to brighten Sam's room.

A shadow cut off the sun outside an instant before the great machine's throaty roar covered all other sounds. Though Gibb had seen a dozen of them so far, he still rushed to the south balcony. Bright March sunlight sparkled off the lander's hull and constantly shifting wings as it floated—like a falling feather on a calm day!—down onto the ocean surface. It was immense. One of the great touring ships could have parked on any of its six wings. On its side, painted large in blue and gold, was the now familiar castle-topped star.

The same design that covered the left breast of the jacket Gibb wore.

But his design was different: atop the starcastle rested a radiant crown, symbol of the imperial family. The Government of Starcastle, as Pip had explained, recognized Gibb's marriage to Samuel Phoe, Grand Duke of Florida. How could it not, Pip had said, under the circumstances that brought about the existence of Starcastle?

Brio had asked Pip, when he mentioned Sam's new title, if it was for service to Starcastle. Pip had laughed, saying, "In all the human universe there are two truly sovereign states: Starcastle and Key West. It would be very rude of me to consider the lands of my Grandfather as conquered!"

Then he had explained what he meant. Auggy Kittmore, the great scientist who gave birth to Starcastle, had loved Sam Phoe most deeply. So much so that he wished to express this love by having children with him, even though such had to be exogenetic and was highly illegal under Corporate Council law. Sam had refused, but Auggy simply stole the cells he needed from Sam. And the genes of these two men created a daughter, Augustina.

In 2616 Augustina Kittmore took control of Auggy's Project Counterweight, also known as Starcastle. The Empress Augustina was Pip's mother. His father was Alexander Kun, last member of the family that had once controlled Glades, during happier times. Starcastle had a strong claim to Florida.

Pip—His Imperial Majesty Alexander II—joined Gibb on the balcony. He placed a large hand on his shoulder. "Sam should be out of bed in a few days, then a week of taking it easy and he'll be back bullying everyone. When things have settled down here, I want you and Sam to visit Starcastle—even Narlo, if he agrees to stop calling himself 'Grand Duchess!'"

Gibb laughed, then nodded enthusiastically.

They stood there for some time listening to the sea and watching the lander unload. Gulls sought an audience, then changed their mind and quickly returned to fish-hunting. Gibb spotted Brio down by the gazebo, adjusting a robot that had tried to place a vertical beam horizontally. He saw them watching, but quickly looked away. Gibb wondered how long the young man would torture himself with thoughts of long-forgiven misdeeds.

Gibb looked sideways at the man beside him, a light breeze tossed his auburn hair. The bright morning sun was already turning his ruddy skin bright pink. World-News had labeled him "Alexander the Greater"—a title that amused Pip.

"Well, much to my regret, it's time to go see Earth's collection of politicians," the Emperor said. "They have no idea that I'm going to put them all out of business in ten years."

"Huh?"

"Starcastle has better things to do than police Earth—we have colony ships circling the planets of two other suns. Vicount Nassel will run the show for five years while we educate the Excludeds and install direct democracy. That's how Starcastle is run most of the time. Comes a war, we dust off the imperial trapping. By twenty-seven thirty, we will withdraw from Earth. Forever, I hope!"

"What about Key West once you leave?"

"Well, the security network we're installing now will make Key West better defended than any city ever has been. Also, I will gladly lease to my royal Grandfather as many regiments of Imperial Guards as the city can afford to feed. Anybody who damages Sam's city will answer to Starcastle. So, on Earth, you will have one global democracy and one very-odd-but-fun grand duchy. It'll work, I think."

The remainder of the day was, for Gibb, a blur of unknown faces and pomp and endless speeches. That he sat beside Pip on a raised dais proved more embarrassment than honor; Gibb wasn't used to so many eyes turned on him—it made his skin crawl. But Pip had insisted: "You represent the new Grand Duchy of Florida!"

And too, he realized, he represented the Peakers and every other tribe of Excludeds destroyed by the cities. With this thought, Gibb straightened his back and coolly returned the stares.

Dawn and the remaining Fundies sat by themselves in one corner of the Plaza. She and Gibb exchanged smiles.

At one point Gibb spotted Russell Makkle, his father.

The man gaped at his son. But only one rather unfair thought ran through Gibb's mind as he watched the man:

You kicked me out—but there's no way in hell you could keep me down!

EPILOGUE

PRIVATE NOTES FOR THE BIOGRAPHY *TWO FATHERS* BY HRH THE PRINCESS GIBBRA (GIBBRA MAKKLE PHOE) WRITTEN AT KEY WEST, 3 AUGUST 2769:

Very likely Gibb Makkle, my father, thought on that day in 2720, when he sat beside an emperor, that he had reached the pinnacle of his life. Such brief fame for him was not to be, however. By the time of his fiftieth birthday, no fewer than nine hundred public buildings, and various streets and plazas, carried his name. And that is only on Earth. How this came about is sad.

In the eighth year Gibb and Sam Phoe were together, five years after their combined genes produced me, Sam vanished. Just as the mysterious Colonel had so many years before, Samuel Phoe simply disappeared without word or trace. Dawn told Gibb that Sam's commander had returned for him. The boy would have listened to her, the man did not. He searched for over a year.

Gibb was devastated. Being only twenty-six then, his emotions hit nadir when all effort at tracing Sam failed. But after a year he found a new lover: the people of Earth. All his waking effort Gibb channeled into making the new worldwide democracy work. He was lucky to be in Key West two months out of any year during the new government's first decade. Jab Ranibi, my godfather, joked once by asking: "How does a man tell if his area of our planet is having its problems? Simple, he discovers Gibb Makkle walking its stony paths." In 2734, Gibb celebrated both his thirty-second birthday and his election as President of the World Council. His was the only inauguration ever attended by an emperor of Starcastle (Alexander III, for Pip had since abdicated in favor of his son in order to join an outbound expedition).

I do not mean to give the impression that my father lived and slept with his state papers, without human touch to his personal needs. Wherever Gibb went, Brio Dirrenni traveled with him. They had become friends; love and marriage followed. They shared many memories. And losses.

The fate of some other people is worth mentioning: Narlo devoted his life during the period before Sam disappeared to adding marble-coated wings onto Whitehead Palace and generally holding court. Yours Truly, as a very little girl, frequently attended, sneezing at the piles of cut flowers that lined his rooms. After Sam's disappearance, Narlo withdrew into himself, seeing few people and living alone in his old apartment. His newest, north, wing of Whitehead Palace stands unfinished to this day.

Dawn emigrated to Starcastle in disgust a few years ago when she at last realized that her son by Gibb, Joel—my half-brother—would never follow her religious footsteps. He teaches humanism beside his master, Jab Ranibi.

Roscoe Thorsel died last year, in his sleep, on his pig farm in Central Florida. His hide was never stripped and fried, as it should have been, because Vicount Nassel needed someone who knew Glades's business dealings in detail so he could sort out who should own what. The Governor General had no intention of rearranging every social pattern on the planet—not in the short time frame Pip had given him.

I can feel your question: *What really happened to Samuel Phoe?* Was my second father murdered by one of his many enemies? Was he lifted directly into heaven by the mysterious Colonel? (Try and tell a New Fundy that he wasn't!)

An informed guess for you, then.

My Father Sam didn't mean to hurt Gibb. Or Narlo for that matter. He simply didn't want his beloved city ruled by a line of absolute monarchs—that is, to continue what he himself already was. I think he removed himself, completely. Oh! he didn't jump off Whitehead Spit into our opaline sea. No, likely he and his grandson Pip are still in suspended animation on their way to a new sun. That's my guess. It would have torn at Sam's heart knowing, as he did, Gibb's reactions; but he always loved Key West first. And in any case, I suspect he knew his young lover well enough to realize that he would recover and would bloom once out of the mayor's shadow. The world attests: He did!

Three years after Sam's disappearance, the Speaker of the Assembly cornered Gibb long enough to ask that he seek Starcastle's approval to assume the ducal title. Gibb refused, saying, "Ask me again when you find Sam's body!"

Gibb knew Sam Phoe's heart.

Today, in the Assembly Hall of the only duchy in history to function without a duke, a bronze statue of Samuel Phoe sits enthroned. Below is a plaque, reading:

THE MAYOR.

There are very few members of that august body who do not truly believe that Sam watches over their shoulders. And any moment might yell "Whale piss!" in their ear at the slightest sign of foolishness.
SAMUEL PHOE, THE MAYOR FOREVER.

William K. Eakins claims the best training for a writer is to become a "generalist" — and he lives by those words with a BA in Psychology, an MS in Environmental Health, and jobs in real estate, county health departments, environmental health, food service inspection and computer programming, not to mention a dozen hobbies from collecting stamps and Roman coins to archaeology, ancient history and camping. In between, he has time to enjoy his Florida home with his lover of 16 years.